The Starfleet Survival Guide has been prepared as a supplement to the standard-issue *Starfleet Basic Survival Manual* that is received by all Starfleet personnel during basic training at Starfleet Academy, and made freely available to all active Starfleet personnel by the Starfleet Bureau of Information. This specialized guide is meant to address unique, unusual, or extremely rare situations that have been encountered by Starfleet personnel, and other explorers of deep space, in recent centuries.

It should be noted that *The Starfleet Survival Guide* does not contain information on basic survival techniques such as those found in the standard-issue *Starfleet Basic Survival Manual. The Starfleet Survival Guide* is intended as a specialized supplement to a basic survival manual, and should not be regarded as a stand-alone survival reference work.

No survival manual ever written can possibly address every situation, crisis, or circumstance that might befall a traveler on an alien world or in deep space. Ultimately, it is the courage, perseverance, and ingenuity of individuals that determines who will be able to adapt and survive.

Good luck.

STAR TREK®

THE STARFLEET SURVIVAL GUIDE

David Mack

ILLUSTRATED BY TIMOTHY M. M. EARLS

Reprinted with permission of the Starfleet Information and Instruction Agency

Document 101321610518-0313

This edition has been modified for security purposes

For distribution only within the United Federation of Planets

POCKET BOOKS
New York London Toronto Sydney Singapore

An *Original* Publication of POCKET BOOKS

POCKET BOOKS, a division of Simon & Schuster, Inc.
1230 Avenue of the Americas, New York, NY 10020

STAR TREK is a Registered Trademark of
Paramount Pictures.

This book is published by Pocket Books, a division of
Simon & Schuster, Inc., under exclusive license from
Paramount Pictures.

ISBN: 0-7434-1842-5

First Pocket Books trade paperback printing September 2002

10   9   8   7   6   5   4   3   2   1

POCKET and colophon are registered trademarks of
Simon & Schuster, Inc.

For information regarding special discounts for bulk purchases,
please contact Simon & Schuster Special Sales at 1-800-456-6798
or business@simonandschuster.com

Printed in the U.S.A.

CONTENTS

1.0

STANDARD-ISSUE EQUIPMENT—
NONSTANDARD USES

1.00   INTRODUCTION

Standard-issue Starfleet equipment has been designed for a high degree of versatility and adaptability. Although Starfleet personnel are well aware that tricorders are multifunction devices of great complexity, we often overlook the myriad capabilities of other personal devices such as phasers and combadges. Often only those officers already tested by experience are aware that onboard systems are capable of much more than their official specification guidelines indicate. Over the past several decades, the Starfleet Corps of Engineers has managed to integrate these systems and devices on a number of levels, yielding a richly interconnected technological whole that far exceeds the capabilities of its discrete components.

1.01   CAUSING LOCALIZED SEISMIC DISRUPTIONS WITH TRICORDER AND/OR COMBADGE SIGNALS

Although creating controlled seismic events is extremely dangerous, they can be an effective deterrent if executed properly—blocking the path of a pursuer or group of pursuers in a wilderness setting by causing the collapse of a large volume of earth, rock, snow, or other material.

This effect is sometimes easy to create with well-placed phaser blasts, but if phasers are not available or have malfunctioned, a variety of terrains might prove susceptible to disruption through the use of ultrasonic and hypersonic signals from a combadge or tricorder. Regions with great quantities of loose rock, muddy earth, or heavy accumulations of snow or similar frozen precipitation can be induced to collapse by using focused sonic waves to reduce their overall strength and cohesion.

For maximum effect, such controlled events should be directed into gullies, narrow canyon passages, or other close areas, providing the greatest degree of obstruction to a pursuer. However, great care should be taken not to execute such a tactic too close to any settled area, or in a location where there is an unacceptably high risk of the controlled event triggering subsequent, uncontrolled events that might lead to unwanted collateral damage.

If the disruption is to be effected using a tricorder:

- Scan the target area for its overall mass and molecular cohesion.

- Press the GEO-1 switch on the tricorder to initialize geological scan protocols.

- Select sense option I for internal sensors, followed by

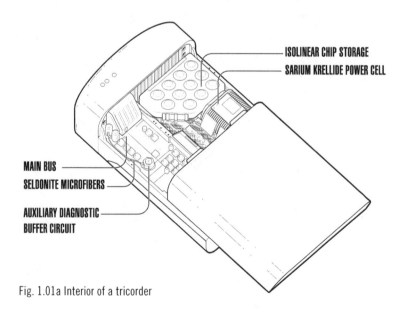

ISOLINEAR CHIP STORAGE
SARIUM KRELLIDE POWER CELL

MAIN BUS
SELDONITE MICROFIBERS

AUXILIARY DIAGNOSTIC
BUFFER CIRCUIT

Fig. 1.01a Interior of a tricorder

command protocol Alpha to set the scan type to the geological mechanics subroutine.

- Run the "GEO Mechanics" subroutine to pinpoint weak areas and zones of maximum stress.

- Select the GEO-2 control to calculate the necessary frequency and amplitude of signal to induce a seismic disruption.

Small volumes of low mass are relatively easy to disrupt with a tricorder; disruptions of greater than 10 metric tons or of highly cohesive material require more power and will necessitate the creation of a collimated signal from the tricorder and any other signal sources immediately available, such as other tricorders and combadges.

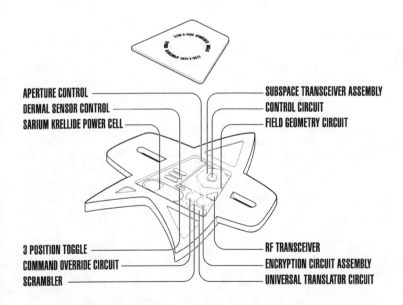

APERTURE CONTROL
DERMAL SENSOR CONTROL
SARIUM KRELLIDE POWER CELL

SUBSPACE TRANSCEIVER ASSEMBLY
CONTROL CIRCUIT
FIELD GEOMETRY CIRCUIT

3 POSITION TOGGLE
COMMAND OVERRIDE CIRCUIT
SCRAMBLER

RF TRANSCEIVER
ENCRYPTION CIRCUIT ASSEMBLY
UNIVERSAL TRANSLATOR CIRCUIT

Fig. 1.01b Interior of a combadge

If the disruption is to be effected using a combadge:

Using a combadge, the process of locating vulnerable areas and selecting appropriate disruption frequencies becomes one of trial and error, with manual adjustments being made through the ultrasonic and hypersonic frequencies until the trigger frequency is found. Caution should be exercised to ensure that while searching for the correct frequency to disrupt the target area, other zones of instability—particularly if they are underfoot or overhead—are not disrupted during the process.

- Open the back access panel and use a fine-grade, non-conductive tool to adjust the RF transceiver—the triangular circuit assembly located below the lower right-hand corner of the subspace transceiver assembly—through its preset frequency and amplitude test series.

- Narrow the transmission bandwidth by adjusting the aperture control, a circular element located at the topmost area of the combadge's internal assembly, to direct the beam.

- Set the signal aperture to a field-of-view (FoV) of approximately .25 to .35 degrees of arc.

- Target the top point of the combadge at the target area.

- Cycle the RF test settings through the ultrasonic and hypersonic frequency ranges until the target area begins to show signs of disruption.

- As soon as disruption effects become visible, leave the RF settings in place and increase the gain to the RF circuit from the combadge's sarium krellide power cell until the desired level of collapse has occurred.

1.02 PROGRAMMING A COMBADGE OR TRICORDER TO TRIGGER PRESET DEVICE EFFECTS AND FUNCTIONS

Most Starfleet personnel are aware that any standard-issue Starfleet device—from a combadge to a tricorder, phaser, or onboard console—can be remotely monitored and deactivated by a properly authorized command routed through an onboard central computer. What is not generally understood, however, is that standard-issue tricorders, combadges, and onboard consoles are capable of initiating or receiving fully integrated command links with other equipment and systems on an independent basis.

Command links can be quickly and easily established with a wide assortment of other Starfleet equipment including, but not limited to, phasers, transporters, force field generators, piloting console functions, and even geological survey mines. This is a tactic that can be very useful in situations where a desired effect must be created quickly and clandestinely.

WITH A COMBADGE

To create a direct command interface between a combadge and another piece of equipment other than an onboard console:

- Open the combadge to reveal its command override circuit. The Command Override Circuit (COC) of the combadge is a small square circuit group located to the immediate left of the encryption circuit assembly. It is activated by pressing its test circuit, which appears as a small circular aperture on the dorsal surface of the COC.

- Press the test circuit.

- Locate the COC of the target device (i.e., the device to be activated by the combadge). In some cases the target COC can be accessed through a software-based command interface (such as with a tricorder or onboard console), and in others must be physically accessed in the same manner as the combadge COC The target device COC is set to "RP" (Receive Protocol) by manipulating the three-position toggle switch on the left side of its assembly to the middle position.

- Move that toggle switch to the middle position. A brief linking pulse is issued from the combadge by double-pressing its COC test circuit. The target device is now primed to receive a triggering command from the combadge.

- Now, set the target device COC to "AP" (action protocol) by changing its toggle switch to the far top position (or selecting the appropriate function from a command interface menu) and specify the action to be triggered by the combadge signal. Any valid function of the target device can be initiated in this manner. (Note that the specified function will not occur while the COC is engaged in AP mode. This is a safety precaution and cannot be overridden.)

- Return the COC to its RP setting and position the target device as necessary. From this point until such time as the device is destroyed or its COC disengaged, a double tap of the command-linked combadge will trigger the specified effect from the target device, provided the target device is within transmission range of the linked combadge.

- When appropriate, double-tap the combadge to trigger the target device.

WITH A TRICORDER

Using a tricorder to create a command link is simpler than using a combadge. Select E for external sensor mode, press Beta to call the "Target Device" submenu, and select the target device. After the correct target device appears on the display screen, engage the target device COC by pressing Alpha to call the command menu, from which you should select the "Command Link" option. Follow the same steps specified above for setting the target device, but use the F1/F2 control function selector to toggle the COC settings, which will appear on the tricorder's display screen.

Once the device is set, the tricorder will offer multiple trigger options: Manual, Countdown, Timed Interval, Proximity, and Conditional. The desired trigger option is selected by pressing the Delta key and activated by pressing the Gamma key.

Manual is used to exercise maximum discretion over the triggering of device effects. A *countdown* can be useful for creating distractions or facilitating tactical requirements in a rigidly timed scenario.

A *timed interval* setting can be set to range from milliseconds to millennia,

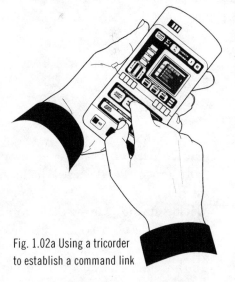

Fig. 1.02a Using a tricorder to establish a command link

Following is a brief list of devices and some of the remote-triggered events that they can be set to execute. This list is by no means exhaustive; it is intended solely to demonstrate the breadth of possibilities created by this dynamic feature of standard-issue Starfleet technology.

- PHASERS: Firing short or long bursts at various power settings; overloading to detonation.

- TRICORDERS: Emitting beacon signals; transmitting prerecorded messages; initiating sonic disruption signals; jamming communications within a short radius.

- TRANSPORTER SYSTEMS: Site-to-site transport on command; Transporter Code 14 (dissociative rematerialization).

- FORCE FIELDS: Activate and deactivate on command, in timed sequence, or in response to specified conditions.

- GEOLOGICAL SURVEY MINES: Detonation.

depending upon the device and the type of effect; this can be useful if the target device is intended to counteract, document, or otherwise capitalize on an event with a known period of recurrence, or to create signal beacons with a regular pattern to facilitate discovery by rescuers.

A *proximity setting* can be used to ward off intruders, defend a perimeter, or otherwise respond to the presence of anyone or anything entering a given range of the device. Note that most devices do not have proximity detection circuits. If the tricorder is left with the target device, however, it can be programmed to act as a proximity circuit.

A *conditional setting* can be used to trigger the device only when specified circumstances are detected, including—but not limited to—an increase or decrease in temperature, immersion of the device in water, or the detection of specified elements above a certain level of concentration within a given range of the device. Most standard-issue devices are not equipped with the necessary hardware or software to execute a conditional

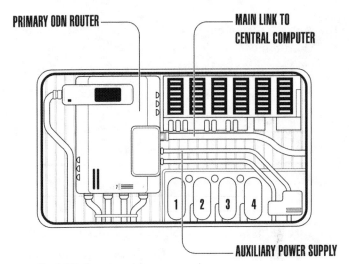

PRIMARY ODN ROUTER

MAIN LINK TO CENTRAL COMPUTER

1 2 3 4

AUXILIARY POWER SUPPLY

Fig. 1.02b Console maintenance panel

setting on their own. In such scenarios a tricorder will have to be left with the target device to fulfill this sensory function.

LINKING TO AN ONBOARD CONSOLE

Linking a tricorder or combadge to an onboard console can be done automatically by requesting a command link from the central computer. If the task needs to be executed manually, follow the same steps specified above for the tricorder or combadge. To manually override the command interface circuit that links the console to the central computer,

- Open the maintenance panel for the console and trace its ODN cables to its primary ODN router. The bundled cable leading out of the router, parallel to the auxiliary power supply, is the main link to the central computer.

- Disconnect this bundle from the router and change the Command Override Circuit (COC) to "Manual." This will enable the COC as the primary control node for the console.

From this point, establishing the interface between the signal device and the target device is the same as specified above.

1.03   PROGRAMMING A TRICORDER TO CONTROL A MEDIUM-RANGE SUBSPACE TRANSMITTER

In the event that normal subspace communications hardware has been rendered inoperative, a combadge and a tricorder can be integrated to act as a short- to medium-range subspace transmitter with a very limited signal gain.

A combadge is typically used only for short-range transmissions between away team members, or for communication with one or more orbiting vessels. As such, its subspace transceiver is not capable of propagating a clear voice signal beyond a range of 500 kilometers.

Standard-issue tricorders, however, possess advanced subspatial sensor packets for use in detecting subspatial and phase-shifted phenomena, and because of their larger power cells they are capable of generating much more powerful signals than combadges. The one function not incorporated into the current tricorder design is a voice transceiver unit (although this is under consideration for the next generation of tricorders being envisioned at Starfleet Research and Development).

By combining the transceiver circuitry of the combadge with the subspatial tracking sensors and superior power reserve of a tricorder, it is possible to fashion a subspace transmitter that can broadcast a single, 5- to 10-second duration, low-resolution audio or raw data signal to a range of up to 1.1 AU.

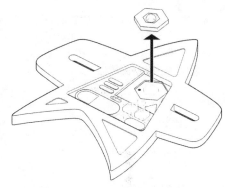

Fig. 1.03a Removing STA from communicator

Because the command menu of a standard-issue tricorder is not currently configured to repurpose the dedicated transceiver circuit of a combadge, the two items must be physically integrated.

- Open the combadge, and carefully remove the transceiver. Great care must be taken because the transceiver circuit is extremely fragile once removed from the combadge shell. The combadge will still be functional after removing the primary transceiver, so long as the auxiliary transceiver in the lower left corner of the combadge is undamaged.

- Install the transceiver into the tricorder using the following protocol:

  ▲ Confirm that the tricorder is deactivated.

  ▲ Open the back panel to reveal the main bus assembly. Near the center of the left edge of the main bus is a .5mm-wide bundle of seldonite microfibers that lead to the auxiliary diagnostic buffer circuit.

  ▲ Remove this circuit, and replace it with the transceiver from the combadge.

▲ Close the back of the tricorder and reactivate the device.

▲ With the reconfigured tricorder now active, select "Download New Subroutine" from the command menu.

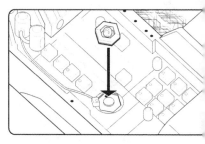
Fig. 1.03b Installing STA into tricorder

▲ Link the tricorder to the combadge, and using the "Download New Subroutine" option, load the combadge's transceiver protocol package into the tricorder.

▲ Run the device's self-diagnostic routine. It will immediately display an error, indicating that the auxiliary diagnostic circuit is misconfigured, and it will ask if you wish to reinitialize the circuit.

▲ Choose yes, and select "New Subroutine" from the initialization submenu. The newly downloaded transceiver protocols will appear in this menu.

▲ Choose "Transceiver Package" and commit to the reinitialization.

▲ When the tricorder prompts you to select a transceiver output node, select the primary subspatial sensor port. It will then ask for a transmission target, with options ranging from General to Encrypted Receiver, and it will ask for a transmission range.

▲ Select a valid receiver within a distance of 1.1 AU.

• Set the tricorder's command override circuit to RP (receive protocol), and set the combadge's COC to AP (action protocol). The tricorder's programmed action will be to engage the newly added transceiver circuit and software package, and emit the subspace signal using its primary subspatial sensor port. This function will be engaged by double-tapping the combadge.

- When appropriate, double-tap the combadge to transmit. It is important to remember that if a subspace signal is being sent to maximum range (1.1 AU) its duration will be less than 5 seconds, and it will be a very weak signal. Voice data might become garbled, and crucial bits of raw data might become lost. Longer messages or data that must be delivered intact should not be sent over distances of greater than .3 AU unless the tricorder can be manually linked to a larger power source, or if the tricorder/combadge assembly is being used solely as the command driver for a powered subspace transmitter that lacks operational software.

If a subspace radio and power source are also available:

In such a case, the tricorder and combadge would be configured in the same manner detailed previously, except that the signal from the tricorder would not be emitted from its primary subspatial sensor port, and an additional subroutine would have to be written to drive the more complex subspace transmitter hardware as part of the tricorder's preset action protocol.

After configuring the combadge and tricorder, disengage the tricorder's internal power supply and then patch the device into the subspace radio control console; the console's EPS tap then is reset to Small Device Interface (to prevent an overload from damaging or destroying the tricorder) and linked directly into the tricorder.

Patch the tricorder's signal output directly into the console's transmitter bus. The newly configured subspace radio should now be ready to transmit a signal of normal strength and data complexity up to its normal maximum range.

1.04 RECONFIGURING A SUBSPACE TRANSCEIVER TO GENERATE A SHORT-DURATION, LOW-POWER FORCE FIELD

With patience and even fairly low-tech tools, any standard-issue combadge can be altered to create a force field of low power and very brief duration.

The key to this modification is to repurpose the low-power subspace field generated by the subspace transceiver assembly (STA). The STA alone is not capable of emitting the force field, however.

- Create an emitter coil, preferably from a conductive metal with low resistance. Metals such as copper and iron, which have been found to be readily available on the vast majority of inhabited planets in known

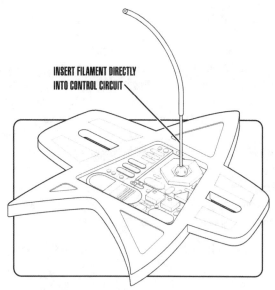

INSERT FILAMENT DIRECTLY
INTO CONTROL CIRCUIT

Fig. 1.04a Attaching monofilament to STA command circuit

space, will prove ideal, but any appropriately conductive element will suffice so long as it can be shaped into a tight coil.

- Expose the STA, taking note of the position of the control circuit—a small circuit in the center of the STA—and the power cell, which should be clearly marked.

- Connect the emitter coil to the control circuit of the STA using an appropriate conductive filament.

- *IMPORTANT! DO NOT ALLOW THE FILAMENT TO CONTACT THE SARIUM KRELLIDE CELL.* In this configuration, the STA is acting as a protective element that prevents overload or shock. *Allowing the filament to make direct contact with the device's power cell while it is connected to the STA could result in a catastrophic, uncontrolled release of energy—i.e., an explosion—or an electric shock powerful enough to kill most humanoids instantaneously.*

- Change the position of the small triangular circuit located to the immediate right of the STA to shape the device's protective energy field. The field can be shaped into a variety of forms, ranging from spherical and hemispherical to conical, planar, curved planar or elliptoid.

A fully charged combadge will be able to generate an energy field with a phase shift of approximately .04 millicochranes for up to 15 seconds. This will prove sufficient to deflect slow physical projectiles (for example, thrown rocks, manually fired arrows, and primitive firearm projectiles) and low-power directed energy attacks (such as those from primitive laser weapons). Faster or significantly more powerful projectiles (such as advanced assault firearms or modern phasers and disruptors) will deplete the force field's energy more quickly or, in some cases, penetrate it with little to no difficulty.

1.05   REMODULATING A UNIVERSAL TRANSLATOR INTO A JAMMING DEVICE

More a commando tactic than a survival technique, using a combadge's universal translator software to scramble a comm circuit is a Starfleet field combat protocol that has been used since 2231.

The universal translator chip (UTC) is an ovoid component located at the bottom right of the comm assembly in a combadge. It is connected by a duranium microfilament to the encryption circuit assembly (ECA). Although the two circuits do not normally exchange information, they are connected in order to facilitate the scrambling of RF transmissions within a radius of 250 kilometers and subspace transmissions within 50 kilometers.

The scrambling function is activated by triggering a switch inside the small circular aperture located above and to the left of the UTC, and below and between the ECA and the Command Override Circuit (COC). Once this switch is triggered, the device's UTC will intercept all RF and subspace transmissions it detects, randomly encrypt them through the ECA, and retransmit them at a boosted power level.

This operation requires a great deal of energy, and that need increases as the number of intercepted signals increases. In a remote area where relatively few signals are being blocked, a fully charged combadge will last for up to an hour. In urban areas or situations in which several signals or a limited number of high-power signals must be blocked, a combadge will last for up to 15 minutes before its energy cells are depleted.

The reason this tactic is often more effective than basic signal interference is that because the Universal Translator is designed to facilitate communication at a conceptual level, it can also be inverted to hinder communication at an equally fundamental level. Essentially, it renders messages unintelligible even between speakers of the same language so that even if the encryption is counteracted, the revealed message will be worthless. This tactic is used on a broader scale by starships, relay stations and orbital devices to enact communications blackouts during periods of civil crisis or war.

A note of caution regarding this tactic is in order, however: Because this function does not discriminate which signals it intercepts and scrambles, Starfleet personnel who employ this protocol will be unable to contact one another or orbiting vessels for the duration of the jamming process, and transporter locks to combadges will likewise be interrupted. Also, if more than one Starfleet crew member is inside the area of effect, personnel from different cultures run the risk of being unable to communicate without the aid of the universal translator. It is imperative that mission directives and rendezvous locations be firmly understood before remote communications are disrupted.

1.06   RECALIBRATING TRANSPORTER ENHANCER ARMBANDS AS TEMPORAL SHIELDS

In scenarios involving temporal disturbances, such as localized distortions of the space-time continuum or zones of fractured pockets of space-time, away teams will require protection from the effects of temporal disruption. One way to devise such protection in the field is to convert a standard-issue Emergency Transporter Armband into a personal temporal shield by modifying it to emit a subspace force field.

Because a temporal shield requires highly sensitive phase discrimination to modulate the subspace force field in response to localized shifts in space-time, the crucial element in the armband modification is its Type VII phase discriminator circuit. This should be adjusted to maximum output in order to provide the best possible protection for its wearer.

The armband's subspace emitter assembly should next be realigned to modulate the discriminated field in an extremely tight configuration around the subject. Keeping the field focused as tightly as possible should permit the subject to interact, on a limited basis, with objects in a temporally disrupted environment.

If more than one away team member is going to enter a temporally disrupted environment, they will not be able to communicate normally because sound waves will not propagate freely through the subspace force field. Communications can be enabled in real time by channeling communicator signals through the Emergency Transport Armband's subspace signal relays, which normally are used to verify transporter signal lock.

In most cases, an Emergency Transport Armband will possess sufficient power to offer basic protection to an average humanoid for approximately 73 minutes. When the modified armband is activated, it will, in essence, create a stabilized pocket of "artificial time" around its subject. In some cases this pocket of artificial time can cause some humanoids to suffer momentary disorientation, and it can adversely affect equilibrium. If symptoms are severe, the armband should be deactivated and removed. In most cases, however, the effects should subside quickly.

It also is important to note that the protection provided by the modified armbands is not total. Prolonged exposure to a temporally disrupted environment, even with the protection offered by a low-power subspace force field, can lead to a rapid onset of temporal narcosis.

Warning signs of temporal narcosis include impaired judgment, irrational behavior, dizziness, loss of balance and motor skills, and eventually panic. Subjects who exhibit symptoms of temporal narcosis should be removed to a temporally stable area as soon as possible.

1.07 REPURPOSING TYPE-1, TYPE-2, AND TYPE-3 PHASERS AS EXPLOSIVE DEVICES

In most tactical situations, photon grenades serve adequately as low-yield, hand-delivered explosives. There are, however, scenarios in which explosives are necessary but grenades are not available. In such an instance, one alternative that many Starfleet personnel have employed to great effect is deliberately inducing an overload in a type-1, type-2, or type-3 phaser, resulting in a powerful detonation.

The design specifications of Starfleet phasers include numerous redundant safety features to prevent accidental overload. The approved methods for energy storage, flow, control, and discharge allow for an amplified rebounding to occur from the storage cell to the prefire chamber, and simultaneously back to the storage cell. While the total energy within the system remains the same, the flow pressure is elevated during the rebound, to the point where the storage cell cannot reabsorb the energy quickly enough. The device's barrier field will be reinforced during this buildup, effectively preventing normal discharge through the emitter. Explosive destruction of the phaser will occur when the energy level exceeds the prefire chamber's density and structural limits.

As the weapon builds up to an overload detonation, conductive acoustic effects will manifest themselves, ranging from 6 kHz to more than 20 kHz within 30 seconds, at a volume level of 41 db at the onset of the overload to 130 db immediately prior to detonation.

The process of inducing an overload is nearly identical in all three versions of this standard-issue Starfleet defensive weapon. The device's safety interlock is intended to prevent overload under most normal operating conditions. The first step for all three phaser types is to disable the safety interlock.

WITH A TYPE-1 PHASER

- Remove the outer casing of the phaser. (illustration 1.07 a) Located beneath the beam intensity and beam width controls is the primary safety interlock assembly. The safety interlock assembly is a code processor for saving the power functions of the phaser and for personalizing a phaser for limited use. It comprises nine circuit assemblies that regulate the functions of the device.

   The largest of these is the prefire control assembly. It is located near the front of the phaser and resembles a long, narrow rectangle.

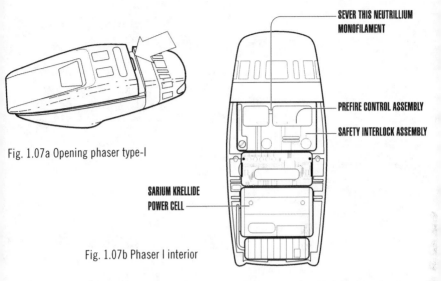

SEVER THIS NEUTRILLIUM MONOFILAMENT

PREFIRE CONTROL ASSEMBLY

SAFETY INTERLOCK ASSEMBLY

Fig. 1.07a Opening phaser type-I

SARIUM KRELLIDE POWER CELL

Fig. 1.07b Phaser I interior

- Deactivate the prefire control assembly by severing the neutrillium monofilament between its two central nodes (Illustration 1.07b). This will prevent the pre-fire chamber from dissipating energy buildup through the phaser's photon spill ports or the emitter crystal.

- Set the beam control assembly to manual override, then replace the phaser casing.

  Follow instructions for all phasers, below.

PHASERS TYPE-2 AND -3

The type-2 phaser contains four prefire chambers, and the type-3 phaser rifle utilizes twelve prefire chambers. Both devices, however, have only one safety interlock assembly, in nearly identical configurations to that of the type-1 phaser. Familiarize yourself with those instructions and follow the same three steps as below:

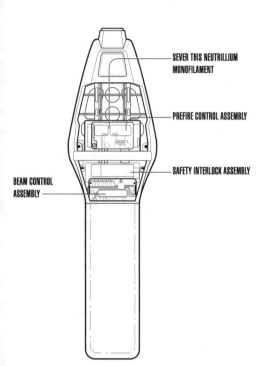

SEVER THIS NEUTRILLIUM
MONOFILAMENT

PREFIRE CONTROL ASSEMBLY

SAFETY INTERLOCK ASSEMBLY

BEAM CONTROL
ASSEMBLY

- Remove the outer casing of the phaser.

- Refer to the accompanying illustrations and deactivate the prefire control circuit. Phaser type-2: illustration 1.07c. Phaser type-3: illustration 1.07d.

- Set the beam control assembly to manual override, then replace the phaser casing.

Fig. 1.07c Phaser II interior

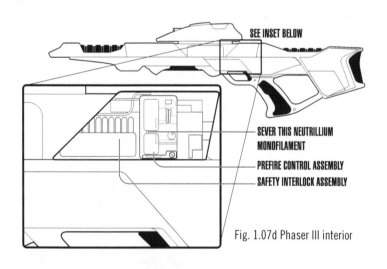

SEE INSET BELOW

SEVER THIS NEUTRILLIUM
MONOFILAMENT

PREFIRE CONTROL ASSEMBLY

SAFETY INTERLOCK ASSEMBLY

Fig. 1.07d Phaser III interior

ALL PHASERS

- Begin the buildup to detonation by setting the phaser's beam intensity to maximum.

- Continue to hold down the beam intensity control until you hear the beginning of the conductive acoustic effect that precedes detonation. Once initiated, the overload cannot be stopped manually, and you will have approximately 30 seconds to reach minimum safe distance from the device.

A type-1 phaser is capable of delivering up to 7.2 million megajoules of explosive force, enough to vaporize three cubic meters of tritanium. In comparison, a type-2 phaser can produce an explosive yield of up to 45 million megajoules, and a type-3 phaser rifle can produce a blast of up to 280 million megajoules—enough to completely destroy a Starfleet runabout.

1.08 STERILIZING FOOD AND WATER WITH A PHASER

In most field survival scenarios, a tricorder is available, and it is relatively easy to scan food supplies and drinking water to verify their purity. Without a tricorder, the worst must always be assumed.

The obvious protocol in most survival situations is to boil water and cook food. In areas without combustible fuel, a well-known method is to use a phaser to heat a rock or piece of salvaged metal until it is glowing with heat energy, then use it to cook food and water.

However, in certain extreme environments, even that "convenience" is unavailable. In a barren desert or arctic region, alternative methods are required to render food and/or water safe for consumption.

Once food has been obtained a phaser can be used to sterilize and cook food directly, after proper precautions are taken.

- Place the food to be sterilized on any clean surface, such as on a strip of uniform fabric; skewered, on a cleaned strip of wood or metal; or suspended from a string or strip of fabric run through a puncture in the food item and held or tied off at either end.

- Set the phaser beam intensity to level 1, and the beam width set to minimum.

- Sterilize the food in sections, at a rate of roughly 3 cubic centimeters per 20 seconds, using a sustained, low-intensity phaser beam.

Food sterilized in this manner should be tested in the manner prescribed in the *Starfleet Basic Survival Manual* before being further cooked or consumed.

It is important not to set the beam intensity too high, or else you will either damage the food at a molecular level, thereby negating its nutritional value, or vaporize it altogether.

SPECIAL CHALLENGES OF AN ARCTIC ENVIRONMENT

In an arctic environment, merely melting snow or ice for drinking water provides no assurance that it is safe to consume. In order to be reasonably assured of its purity, it is necessary to boil it before considering it safe. Without a container to hold the water while it is boiling, this can seem to be a daunting task. The key is to not attempt to immediately shift the water from a frozen state to a boiling temperature, but rather to effect a gradual change in temperature.

- Use a phaser to excavate an area, capable of holding several dozen liters of water, out of the deep snow cover or thick surface ice. This can be achieved quickly with a relatively high beam intensity and a broad beam width. Rapidly heating the snow or ice into a gaseous state should leave behind a wet, roughly concave surface.

- Allow this surface to refreeze.

- Refill this concavity with loose snow or chipped ice fragments. Do not pack the snow or ice into the space too tightly.

- Set the phaser to beam intensity level 1 and beam width level 2.

- From a distance of less than one meter, slowly melt the snow or ice fragments with 10-second sustained beams, separated by 3 seconds of cool-down time for the phaser's emitter crystal. Be careful not to sustain the beam for too long, or you will risk causing a phaser overload.

- Keep the beam moving slowly across the surface area of the ice fragments or snow to ensure an even melt. This should require no more than three sustained phaser discharges.

- Once the ice or snow has melted completely, adjust the phaser's settings to beam intensity 2, beam width 4.

- From point-blank range, keep the beam directed into the water, in 10-second bursts, followed by 3-second cool-down periods.

- Continue to do this until the water begins to give off thin wisps of water vapor. This should occur after no more than 3 discharges. At the first sign of water vapor,

- Reset the phaser to beam intensity 3, beam width 7, and place the emitter crystal into the water approximately one centimeter below the surface. A single 15-second discharge should be sufficient to raise the temperature of 12 liters of water to the boiling point.

As the water cools, it can be safely consumed or used for cooking. It can also be allowed to refreeze, at which time it can be cut into small segments for easy portability if insulated water containers are unavailable, and remelted as necessary.

1.09 CHARGING A SHUTTLE BATTERY OR SHIP'S CONSOLE WITH A TYPE-1, TYPE-2, OR TYPE-3 PHASER POWER CELL

One of the most dynamic and widely used power sources for Starfleet equipment and small spacecraft is the sarium krellide power cell. It is employed in various sizes and configurations in everything from combadges and phasers to shuttlecraft power plants and onboard console assemblies.

Sarium krellide power cells normally are recharged through standard taps of a starship or starbase's electroplasma system, and in the field through bulk sarium krellide units. In crisis scenarios, however, a downed shuttlepod might require a recharging of its onboard sarium krellide cells when standard sources are unavailable. A slow, tedious, and often dangerous emergency tactic in such cases is to transfer the energy from a phaser's sarium krellide cell to the shuttlecraft's by means of a controlled, direct current beam.

The complicating factor of this procedure is that, because standard-issue sarium krellide cells are designed only to be recharged through the EPS taps, physical modifications are required to both the phaser and the recharging node of the destination power cell.

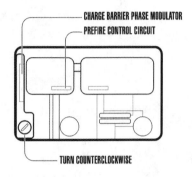

CHARGE BARRIER PHASE MODULATOR
PREFIRE CONTROL CIRCUIT

TURN COUNTERCLOCKWISE

POWERING A SHUTTLE BATTERY

Fig. 1.09a The safety interlock assembly

First, prepare the phaser:

- Remove the phaser's outer casing to expose the safety interlock assembly (SIA).

    The narrow assembly located to the far left side of the SIA is the prefire control circuit.

- Adjust the prefire control circuit to change the phase modulation of the prefire chamber's collapsible charge barrier. The charge barrier phase modulator is located at the top of the prefire control circuit, and should be adjusted counterclockwise until the nadion pulse output is stabilized. This will transform the phaser's rapid nadion output into a stable, directed current.

    Once the phaser has been adjusted, the recharging port of the destination power cell must be primed.

- Remove its outer node casing to reveal the LiCu 521 receptor crystal. Its default aperture setting is minimum arc. The control to reset its aperture is located immediately below the crystal.

- Move the control to the right to reset the acceptable aperture to maximum. This adjustment will allow the receptor crystal to compensate for minor fluctuations in beam stability that will occur during transfer from a handheld device instead of a static EPS port.

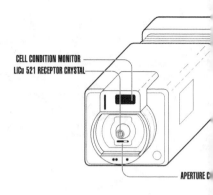

CELL CONDITION MONITOR
LiCu 521 RECEPTOR CRYSTAL

APERTURE C

Fig. 1.09b A shuttle's power cell with EPS receptor crystal cover removed

- Using the phaser's safety interlock assembly, reduce its beam intensity settings by 75 percent. This is necessary to ensure that the receptor crystal is not overloaded during transfer, and to minimize the risk of damaging sensitive components around the receptor crystal assembly in the event of an accident that should cause the beam to be directed off its mark.

- Finally, secure the phaser's emitter crystal as close as possible to the destination cell's receptor crystal without actually allowing the two crystals to make physical contact. IMPORTANT! Be sure that the two crystals do not come into contact. Because they are composed of the same ultradense, ultrahard composite, there is a risk that one or both crystals could sustain microscopic scratches or other damage if they come into contact. Such damage could result in dangerous

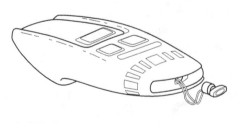

Fig 1.09c Removing a phaser's emitter crystal

feedback loops that would lead to a rapid overload of one or both devices.

- Set the phaser to minimum beam intensity and width. A continuous beam should be discharged directly into the destination cell's receptor crystal.

It will take approximately 30 minutes to drain a fully charged type-1 phaser in this manner. A fully charged type-2 phaser can be drained in approximately 3.5 hours. A fully charged type-3 phaser rifle can be drained in approximately 13 hours. A standard shuttlecraft's three onboard sarium krellide cells can each be charged to a capacity of 5.6×10^8 MJ. It would take 78 type-1 phasers to recharge a single onboard power cell. It would require only 13 type-2 phasers, and only two type-3 phaser rifles, to accomplish the same task.

A Starfleet shuttlecraft carrying two passengers can escape Earth-normal gravity, transmit a general subspace S.O.S., and maintain life support for up to 90 minutes on one fully charged sarium krellide cell.

POWERING AN ONBOARD CONSOLE

Establishing a conection between a phaser's sarium krellide cell and the primary power input for an onboard console is a delicate task, and one that should be attempted under only the most dire circumstances. The risk of electrocution is extremely great, and the potential for catastrophic feedback into the phaser's power cell is significant.

This procedure is predicated on the assumption that the systems linked to the console in question still have power and are functioning correctly, and the need for an alternative power cell is the result of the console's power supply having been inter-

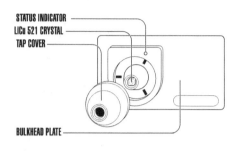

STATUS INDICATOR
LiCu 521 CRYSTAL
TAP COVER

BULKHEAD PLATE

Fig. 1.09d Diagram of EPS tap

rupted from a remote location. An example of this would be a transporter console whose power has been cut off, although its attendant transporter system is still powered and functional.

- Remove the phaser's outer casing to reveal its safety interlock assembly and emitter crystal.

- Adjust the prefire control circuit to remodulate the collapsible charge barrier so that it regulates the rapid nadion pulse into a stable directed energy flow, as above.

- Cautiously remove the phaser's LiCu 521 emitter crystal. Be careful not to damage its connection to the prefire chamber.

- Locate an EPS recharging tap.

- Open it and remove the protective casing surrounding the recharger node.

- Remove the recharger safety interlock assembly to reveal the recharging node crystal.

- Manually override its EPS power supply and select "Interrupt." When the green indicator light above the

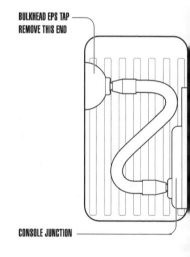

BULKHEAD EPS TAP
REMOVE THIS END

CONSOLE JUNCTION

Fig. 1.09e A console's EPS junction

recharger crystal goes out, the connection is no longer live. You may now safely

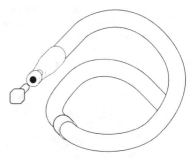

- Detach the recharger crystal from its EPS power cable.

- Go to the console you wish to remotely power and open its maintenance panel.

Fig 1.09f Attaching an EPS receptor crystal to the console's EPS line

- Locate the EPS supply cable and detach the end of the cable connected to the bulkhead EPS tap. Do not disconnect the cable from the console power input node.

- Attach the free end of the console's power supply cable to the back of the recharger crystal. Then

- Secure the front edge of the recharger crystal into the phaser's beam emitter assembly, directly in front of the prefire chamber.

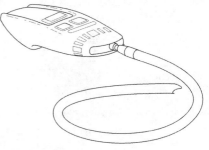

- Set the phaser's beam intensity to 75 percent of maximum and its beam width to minimum.

Fig. 1.09g Securing the recharge crystal to the phaser's beam emitter

- Adjust the phaser's safety interlock controls to maintain continuous discharge until the device is drained.

A type-1 phaser should be able to power a standard Stafleet onboard console for up to 3 minutes. A type-2 phaser can power the same console for up to 15 minutes, and a type-3 phaser rifle should provide up to a full hour of continuous power.

1.10   PROTECTING A CAMPSITE FROM PESTS, USING A TRICORDER AND PHASER

On many planets, indigenous fauna pose particular hazards to away teams and other explorers. The vast majority of the galaxy's animal and insect species have not been catalogued, which can make it difficult to develop effective deterrents against those species that are capable of killing or inflicting serious injury upon humanoids.

As detailed in the *Starfleet Basic Survival Manual*, standard-issue insect repellents and basic tactics—such as building a hot, smoky fire—will repel most animal pests. However, there often are scenarios in which it is either not possible or not advisable to ignite a fire. In addition, some species of insects have proved to be unaffected by standard repellent formulas, and certain dangerous animal life-forms are actually attracted to fire and other light sources.

One often effective alternative method is to use a tricorder to generate animal- and insect-repelling signals that are not audible to humanoid species.

TO REPEL INSECTS

- Use the tricorder to isolate as many different insect and nonsentient animal species as possible within a 200-meter radius. Many insect species communicate by means of specific types and frequencies of sound.

Use the tricorder to isolate all the detected insect sound emissions into discrete signals.

- Use the tricorder's universal translator circuit to interpret the insects' natural vocabulary, then program it to emulate signals that are shown to cause the insects to retreat. The tricorder is capable of mimicking more than 1,000 unique subaural signatures simultaneously. Ideally, more than one tricorder will be available; if so, upload the signal data from the first tricorder to all the others. Program all available tricorders to continually transmit the repellent signals. This should be sufficient to deter the vast majority of insect species from approaching the camp perimeter.

If only one tricorder is available:

- Make camp at the highest reachable safe position, as far from water and thick vegetation as possible.

- Clear excess vegetation from the camp. Place the tricorder approximately 9 meters from the camp perimeter, preferably at a lower elevation.

LARGER ANIMAL SPECIES

Dealing with larger animal species can be more problematic. Whereas insect species are often easy to manipulate through harmless electronic and infrared signals, many animal species—particularly predators—can be far more difficult to deter.

- Begin by employing the same tactics used against the insects. Scan for animal sounds—mating calls, warning calls, etc. Use the tricorder's universal translator to process the animals' vocabularies. (The universal translator is as adept at parsing simple, primitive language forms as it is at deciphering complex sentient languages. This feature of the universal translator is often overlooked by personnel in the field.)

- After different animal species' signatures are discerned, experiment with varying subaural frequencies to determine which signals, if any, will nonviolently repel nearby animals.

If more than one tricorder is available, you might consider placing them at intervals equidistant from your base camp. Keep in mind that your tricorder is one of the most valuable tools at your disposal. NEVER leave your tricorder unattended. Always evaluate your risk and use your resources wisely. All reasonable precautions, such as chemical repellants, artificial shelters and/or building a fire, should still be employed if possible.

1.11 SURVIVING ATMOSPHERIC REENTRY IN A PRESSURE SUIT

Atmospheric reentry without the benefit of a craft designed for the purpose is one of the most palpably dangerous activities imaginable. In addition to the risks posed by atmospheric friction, making planetfall without a vessel is especially hazardous. Despite these risks, orbital skydiving continues to be a popular activity, but orbital skydiving is accomplished through the use of specially designed jumpsuits that contain features not found on standard EVA equipment.

In an emergency situation that requires abandoning a craft by evacuating into space while in orbit, the first objective—after reaching minimum safe distance from the abandoned craft—will be to remain in orbit until help arrives. The Starfleet standard extravehicular work garment (SEWG) is equipped with an automated, short-range subspace distress signal beacon, as well as reinforced pressure and radiation layers, a 16-hour consumables supply, and enhanced recycling features. The SEWG offers the wearer essentially unlimited micrometeoroid and radiation protection, and its life-support functions are fully autonomic. In any scenario in which the subspace distress beacon has been activated and help can be expected to arrive in less than 24 hours, a stranded individual should strive to remain spaceborne.

In circumstances when help is not expected to arrive within a survivable time frame, it might be desirable to attempt planetfall in order to reach an environment capable of extending survival. Numerous details about a planet will determine whether such a course of action is prudent: the presence of breathable atmosphere; surface geography, particularly the presence of an ocean or other deep body of water; gravity; and geologic stability are just some of the essential factors that need to be evaluated when gauging the relative safety of a given planet.

For instance, making planetfall to a world lacking a breathable atmosphere can be more dangerous than remaining in orbit; descending in an EVA suit to a planet with a corrosive atmosphere would be tantamount to suicide. A planet rife with volcanic activity, or one which has extremely high gravity, would likely be too dangerous an environment in which to survive while awaiting rescue. Similarly, a planet that lacks an ocean or other deep body of water to cushion the landing will be unsuitable for an unprotected landing in a SEWG, which lacks thrusters or a parachute to slow its descent.

If the destination planet is deemed suitable for landing, the protocol for initiating descent must be followed closely. A Starfleet SEWG is not designed for atmospheric reentry, but it can be modified in extreme circumstances to maximize the odds of survival. It should be noted that a Starfleet low-pressure environment garment (LPEG), which appears very similar to a SEWG, is intended only for benign airless operations, and will not by itself provide sufficient protection to attempt an unshielded planetfall. Even with a properly modified SEWG, the odds of surviving an unshielded atmospheric reentry are minimal at best.

The first and most crucial preparation to make to the SEWG in anticipation of planetfall is to modify the sub-space transceiver assembly in the two forearm control interfaces to generate a subspace forcefield. This is necessary because a SEWG, unlike a dedicated orbital skydiving garment (OSG), is not armored with ablative plating nor insulated with nitrogen-cooled tritanium mesh, which enable the wearer of the OSG to endure the rigors of atmospheric friction.

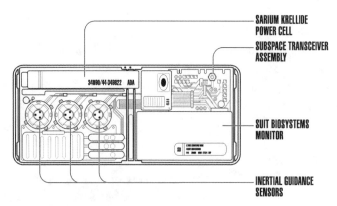

Fig. 1.11a A typical forearm control interface

To create the subspace force field:

- Power down the forearm control interfaces, then open them to reveal their subspace transceiver assemblies (STAs).

- From inside the SEWG's left-leg storage pocket, remove the tether cable, which is used to help connect two or more space-walking individuals for mutual safety.

- Remove the protective outer layer of the cable to reveal the inner triple coil of elastic kelvinium fiber. The kelvinium coil can serve as an emitter coil once it is connected to the sarium krellide cells and STAs.

- First unravel the triple coil at one end of the tether.

- Using the laser-welder from the SEWG's standard repair kit, fuse one thread of kelvinium coil to the STA's control circuit, which appears as a small, circular feature in the center of the STA.

- Fuse the other two coils of the kelvinium tether to the STA's grounding circuit.

- After one end of the tether is attached, loop the tether around the torso, over one shoulder, behind the back and up over the opposite shoulder, forming an "X" across the back.

- Unravel the coil at the free end of the tether, and fuse it to the STA control circuit and grounding circuit on the free arm, in the same manner described above.

  It is important that once the kelvinium coil is attached to the STA that it not be allowed to contact the forearm control interfaces' exposed sarium krel-lide power cells. Doing so could result in an uncon-trolled and catastrophic release of energy of sufficient intensity to disintegrate the SEWG and its wearer.

- Once the coil is solidly connected to both STAs, pro-gram the SEWG's built-in computer to remotely adjust the forearm control interface STAs' phase modulation by .08 millicochranes, and adjust their subspace field geometry from narrow-band to inverse parabolic.

- Reroute the SEWG's remaining power cells to the forearm STAs, excepting for the cell that powers the subspace distress beacon.

    Do not power up the forearm STAs until after atmospheric penetration has begun. Activating the STAs too soon will prematurely deplete their power supply.

Initiate a controlled descent:

- Aim toward a large body of water by using short, con-trolled releases of pressurized exhaust gas from the SEWG's airscrubber tank.

- Maintain as shallow an angle of descent as possible.

    The optimum angle of descent varies based on each planet's specific gravity and atmospheric density and composition. As a general rule, however, the steeper the angle of descent, the greater the degree of friction and the greater the heat that will build up against the SEWG. Fortunately, fluid dynamics favor a blunt aerodynamic profile during a reentry sce-nario, and the SEWG's ability to withstand radiation and micrometeroid impacts will help it resist most

Fig. 1.11b Proper position for atmospheric entry

upper atmosphere reactive and nonreactive molecular collisions.

- When the descent begins to produce such discernible thermal effects around the SEWG as visible gas-surface interactions or an energetic and highly ionized flow impact buffer, power up the STAs in the forearm control interfaces.

- Turn your back toward the planet and bring your arms, legs, and head as close to the center of your body as possible as you continue to descend.

The subspace force field generated by the STAs will be focused in a shallow, convex field behind your back, protecting you from the majority of the thermal effects associated with atmospheric reentry. Residual radiation associated with reentry will be absorbed by the SEWG.

- Maintain the protective position until the thermal effects subside.

Note that planets with exceptionally dense atmosphere or high gravity—or worse, both—will result in a greater amount of friction for a longer duration. Penetration of the upper levels of atmosphere is the second-most vulnerable phase of an unprotected reentry scenario. If the sarium krellide cells of the SEWG become depleted before the thermal effects of reentry subside, you will be vaporized almost instantly.

If atmospheric penetration is successful and you have achieved freefall:

- Immediately power down the STAs.

The next challenge will be to reach the surface of the planet alive and with a minimum of injury. An OSG is equipped with a combination thruster pack and parachute to facilitate landing on a variety of terrain. A SEWG typically is not equipped with either of those features, so a different approach is required. The duration of a freefall from a planet's upper atmosphere to its surface varies based on atmospheric depth and density and the planet's gravity, but in most cases you will have between three minutes and seven minutes to prepare for splashdown.

During this time:

- Use the SEWG's built-in computer to change the subspace field geometry of the forearm STAs from inverse parabolic to the narrowest possible field around the SEWG itself. This will serve to change the subspace force field from a shield configuration to one that most closely resembles a starship's structural integrity field.

- Reroute all remaining power to the forearm STAs, and

- Set the gain on the sarium krellide cells to maximum.

Do not activate the STAs until the last possible moment.

- Use the descent phase to control your splashdown point as best you can. Aim for a point between 3 kilometers and 5 kilometers from a shoreline to improve the likelihood that the water will be deep enough to cushion your impact and still place you close enough to land to swim ashore.

Approximately 10 seconds before splashdown, activate the STAs and once again gather your limbs as close in to your body as possible; try to hit the water with your feet and buttocks (or equivalent anatomy).

If the SEWG has sufficient remaining power, the subspace force field may be able to shield you from the bulk of the impact, but you will most likely suffer a stunning level of deceleration trauma in any event.

If the SEWG's power supply has been depleted, you will be killed on impact.

If you survive splashdown and the suit has any power reserves remaining, power down the STAs and set the SEWG to low-power mode as you proceed to shore.

Conserve your energy by swimming underwater rather than fighting against surface wave motion, and rely on the SEWG's air supply.

If the SEWG's breathable air reserves are depleted you will need to shed the entire suit at sea before swimming to shore. In that circumstance, reroute all remaining power to the subspace distress beacon and activate it before abandoning the suit. This may summon help and could provide search parties with a starting point from which to initiate rescue operations.

Once you are in the water, remember to apply all open-sea survival protocols as detailed in the *Starfleet Basic Survival Manual*. Be particularly aware of aquatic predators, and let currents help you if at all possible.

The comm system of a SEWG is extremely limited in its range. It generally is intended for use only on the exterior of a starship or space station, or on an away mission to a hostile environment while a support vessel remains nearby or in orbit. In an emergency scenario in which a SEWG's short-range subspace beacon does not have adequate range to signal a nearby starship or starbase, the comm circuits of two SEWGs can be interplexed to generate a much more powerful subspace carrier wave on a variety of Starfleet frequencies.

Interplexing the comm systems of two or more SEWGs can be accomplished quickly and easily by setting uplink and override protocols through the SEWGs' forearm control interfaces. The one major drawback to this technique is that overriding the signal-gain capacitor by interplexing the comm units makes modulation of the signal's content nearly impossible. The resulting signal generated by a pair of interplexed SEWG comm circuits will be powerful, but might be interpreted as random subspace noise.

Another significant risk is that interplexing the comm circuits of two or more SEWGs creates a risk that all the interplexed comm systems might be damaged, compromising their ability to focus long-range transmissions. Consequently, multiple transmissions of an interplexed signal might prove difficult or impossible. If it is possible, however, a series of brief signal bursts in groupings meant to represent the prime numbers 3, 5, and 7 will maximize the likelihood that the signals will be recognized as intentional rather than random.

1.12 RECONFIGURING TRANSPORTERS TO CREATE PERPETUAL STASIS LOOPS

In extremely bleak survival scenarios in deep space, it is possible to reconfigure a transporter system to store a quantum-level pattern for very long periods of time. Storing patterns in a transport buffer is extremely risky; a loss of power, physical damage to the transporter system, or such phenomena as ion storms or magneton pulses can all compromise the integrity of a quantum-level signal. In addition, if all the surviving members of a ship's crew are placed into stasis, the ship will effectively be left unmanned and highly vulnerable to hostile incursion. Be positive that certain criteria are met before attempting this extreme approach to survival.

First, the ship or facility where you are stranded should be all but exhausted of such consumable supplies as food, water, and breathable atmosphere. All attempts to signal for help should be made before switching over to an automated distress beacon and entering stasis. It also is important that every viable attempt at escape be explored before choosing this alternative.

Only if all the above criteria have been met and there is no reason to believe that help will arrive within the expected duration of survival should you attempt transporter stasis.

The procedure for modifying the transporter system is fairly straightforward. The following steps should be repeated for every transporter console that needs to be modified.

- Begin by rerouting all primary and auxiliary power to the transporter systems. (Starfleet automated distress beacons are powered by dedicated fusion cells, and will not be affected by this transfer of power allocation.)

- Access the command override protocols for the transporter console and disable the rematerialization subroutine and its redundant fail-safe backups.

- Connect the phase inducers to the emitter array; this will allow the phase inducers to act as a regenerative power source, and they also will compensate for minor quantum variances in signal integrity.

- On the underside of the transporter console, open the maintenance panel and physically remove the override circuits. This will prevent the console's automated diagnostic routines from disabling your modifications.

- Return to the main transporter control interface and access the command routines for the pattern buffer.

- Lock the pattern buffer into a continual Level One diagnostic to monitor and maintain pattern integrity. This will engage the phase inducers to route the matter array through the buffer, maintaining the closest possible quantum balance between the subject's matter and energy signatures.

If you are placing other individuals into transporter stasis, dematerialize them individually, taking care to assign only one person to each pattern buffer.

If you are placing yourself into transporter stasis, set an automated dematerialization routine with a delay period sufficient to allow yourself to move from the console to the transporter platform.

It is important to note that humanoids held in transporter stasis are not aware of the passage of time. If your attempt at stasis is successful, it will seem from your point of view to be no different from an ordinary transport cycle.

This complex and highly innovative solution to long-term survival was devised in 2294 by Captain Montgomery Scott, former chief engineer of the starships *U.S.S. Enterprise* NCC-1701 and *U.S.S. Enterprise* NCC-1701-A. Captain Scott and a young Starfleet officer, Ensign Matt Franklin, were the only two survivors of the crash of the transport vessel *Jenolen*, which impacted on the surface of a Dyson Sphere while en route to the Norpin V Colony.

When Captain Scott and Ensign Franklin realized that they had no means of signaling for assistance, and that the *Jenolen* had no consumable supplies to sustain them while awaiting rescue, Captain Scott hit upon the ingenious notion of storing a living being's quantum pattern in the transporter pattern buffer.

Captain Scott had anticipated a rescue within a matter of months, but he wisely configured the pattern-storage matrix to sustain his and Franklin's patterns for much longer if necessary. As it turned out, his decision proved fortuitous; the wreck of the *Jenolen* was not discovered until 75 years later, by the starship *U.S.S. Enterprise* NCC-1701-D. Captain Scott's pattern survived its long period in stasis with only a .003 percent degradation of signal integrity. Unfortunately, the pattern of Ensign Franklin degraded by more than 53 percent because of a failure of the phase inducer that was sustaining his quantum signal, and the *Enterprise* away team was unable to recover his pattern.

Despite the tragic loss of Ensign Franklin, Captain Scott successfully demonstrated that it is possible to preserve high-resolution matter-energy signatures in long-term transporter stasis. Since his rescue from the *Jenolen*, the principles he pioneered have been refined by the Starfleet Corps of Engineers, who are planning to build a transporter designed specifically to hold patterns in dematerialized stasis for long journeys across intergalactic distances. If feasible, such developments may help facilitate exploration of the universe beyond the Milky Way Galaxy.

1.13   USING HOLODECK DATA CORES TO SAVE TRANSPORT PATTERNS

Federation transporters are equipped with multiple redundant fail-safes, making them highly reliable and extraordinarily safe. However, because transporter systems are extremely complex and designed to handle highly energetic and complex quantum-level operations, when errors do arise they can be unpredictable and severe.

A transporter signal is very vulnerable to decay and dissolution if it is not reassembled immediately. In the event that an isolated transporter system suffers a catastrophic failure after dematerializing living subjects—which require quantum-level resolution of both their physical forms and energy states—it is crucial that the data be preserved until such time that the physical patterns and energy-state data can be reintegrated. However, this can be a daunting task, because storing the quantum energy state of even a single living being as raw data can overwhelm a medium-capacity computer core.

In order to save living subjects' energy states as data, the computer storage volume of an entire starship or small starbase will be required. (The computers of a runabout, for example, would be insufficient to store the quantum energy state of even a single humanoid.) To prime the computers for their task, execute a priority command override to wipe as much computer memory—from all systems shipwide or stationwide—as is necessary to store the quantum energy data. Keep in mind that this will not affect locked core partitions, dedicated systems operating independently of the main computer system, or protected backup media, which can be used to restore core systems at a later time.

Physical matrix patterns are easier to preserve if they can be routed to a system that is designed specifically to store and manipulate complex physical structures and energy signatures. Holodeck and holosuite memory core interfaces are ideal for this task. However, using a holodeck or holosuite system to store physical patterns poses two critical risks:

1. If programs are active in the holographic matrix when the physical patterns are stored there, they will overwrite the physical patterns of holoprogram characters currently in the active memory buffer. This means that damage inflicted upon bodies stored in this manner will persist when the physical pattern is reintegrated with its quantum energy signature. If a character is killed or otherwise eliminated from the story path of an active program, the program will purge the character and its physical template from active memory, erasing the stored physical pattern at the same time, making it impossible to reconstitute the lost individual's pattern. For this reason, it is important not to shut down, erase, interrupt, or purge any holoprogram that is running when the patterns are saved. Examples of interruptions that can damage the patterns in the memory buffer would be a loss of power to the holographic matrix, or calling for the doors or control interfaces. Either of these actions can disrupt the integrity of the holographic imaging array.

2. Although holoprograms are maintained in the active memory buffer, holoprogram safety protocols and mortality fail-safes are part of the primary computer core's command directory. These safety precautions—which in theory prevent a holographic scenario from intentionally inflicting real harm or lethal force against living participants—will no longer be

available because they have been overwritten by the storage of the quantum energy signatures in the primary memory core.

To reintegrate physical patterns stored in a holographic matrix with their quantum energy signatures and successfully rematerialize them will require an independent computer core with a protected operating system, and a fully functional dedicated transporter system. Because software essential to data transfer might be compromised during the initial overwriting of information to save the patterns, a hard patch between the storage core and the core used to direct reintegration and assembly is strongly recommended.

This rather extreme and original solution to the crisis of a failed transporter system was developed in 2371 by Lieutenant Commander Michael Eddington of Starfleet, while he was serving aboard space station Deep Space Nine. The *Runabout Orinoco*, returning from a routine journey, fell prey to sabotage and was destroyed. Eddington beamed the crew of the *Orinoco* out of the vessel in time, but a surge of charged antimatter particles compromised the transporter's annular confinement beam, leading to a catastrophic overload in the transporter's energizing coils.

In a matter of seconds, as the signals of the officers in the pattern buffer teetered on the edge of dissolution, Eddington acted quickly to transfer their signal data into the computer systems of the station. Fortunately, the computer automatically routed the physical patterns to the holosuite memory core because the signal data conformed so closely to the programs normally configured for that system.

Deep Space Nine chief medical officer Lieutenant Julian Bashir was in the holosuite running an espionage-related recreational program, and he risked his own life to preserve the safety of his fellow officers by prolonging the program's operation until Eddington and the Deep Space Nine engineering crew managed to establish a hard connection between the station's computers, the holosuite memory core, and the systems aboard the *U.S.S. Defiant*. Fortunately, all five passengers of the *Orinoco* were rematerialized unharmed.

1.14 TRANSMITTING CODED SUBSPACE SIGNALS BY ADJUSTING A WARP DRIVE'S FIELD PHASE COILS

There are numerous scenarios in which a Starfleet officer might need to send a covert subspace signal from a hostile environment. When one is held aboard a warp-capable starship, a unique opportunity for sending coded signals presents itself.

In most cases, communications systems aboard alien starships will be security restricted, and without special equipment, software, and training it will be all but impossible to access them. However, an officer trained in even basic computer science should be able to access the secondary, nonessential systems of most vessels. An ideal target for subtle tampering is a vessel's warp field phase adjustment circuits, which are used to suppress characteristic subspace static caused by the operation of warp coils.

By establishing a simple oscillation in the subspace field masking algorithm, a short repetitive pulse-type signal can be encoded into the background static of a vessel's warp signature.

Two other system types that might prove vulnerable to this kind of adjustment are shield-harmonic regulators, and secondary navigational sensor palettes. Modifying these systems is not as likely to be successful as altering the warp field phase adjustment coils, however, because they are not used as consistently. The shield harmonic regulators will produce a detectable signal only when the vessel's shields are activated, and to transmit a signal via the secondary navigational sensors, the primary navigational sensors will first have to be disabled. Doing so might draw undesired attention to an officer in a covert operation. It might also prompt a more thorough precautionary scan of the secondary systems in order to prevent further sabotage, thereby exposing the signal modifications.

This ingenious signalling method was devised in 2366 by Commander William T. Riker, first officer of the *U.S.S. Enterprise*-D. Riker was abducted from the surface of Betazed, along with *Enterprise* counselor Lieutenant Commander Deanna Troi and her mother, Lwaxana Troi of Betazed, by DaiMon Tog, commander of the Ferengi Marauder *Krayton*.

Riker, unable to access the *Krayton*'s communications array, successfully modified the Ferengi starship's warp field phase adjustment with an oscillation that mimicked the unique tempo of Algolian ceremonial rhythms that had been performed aboard the *Enterprise* only a few days prior to his abduction.

Enterprise personnel, investigating the kidnapping from orbit over Betazed, detected the distinctive rhythmic patterns concealed in the Ferengi vessel's cochrane distortion, and were able to use the signal to intercept the *Krayton* shortly thereafter.

The important goal in such an action is to create a signal that will be recognizable to its intended recipients but will appear as nothing more than random static to other parties. This is most effective when a signal is prearranged, but a variety of effective signal types can be devised extemporaneously.

Recommended signal types might include unique musical tempos, antiquated binary signal forms, or numeric series. Other effective signal types will no doubt suggest themselves based on our own experience, intended signal recipient, and the type of hostile forces being dealt with.

1.15   SEALING QUANTUM FISSURES WITH AN INVERTED WARP FIELD

Although a quantum fissure sounds like a submicroscopic phenomenon, its name is misleading. A quantum fissure can extend across a moderate distance of space-time, and it represents a serious threat not only to vessels that encounter it directly, but to the universe as a whole.

A quantum fissure is a fixed point in the space-time continuum that acts as an intersection between an infinite number of possible quantum realities. When a warp-capable vessel comes into contact with a quantum fissure, warp fields can cause a rupture in the natural subspace barrier between quantum realities. Subjects that pass through the resulting rupture are forced into a state of quantum flux, resulting in unpredictable episodes of shifting between realities.

If parallel realities overlap or intersect on a large enough scale, the resulting effects could disrupt the universal energy constant and contribute to a radically accelerated end state of either an endothermic or exothermic nature. Worse, as parallel realities overlap and intersect, some might be annihilated by the interaction of matter with diametrically opposed quantum states. Innumerable realities would be permanently destroyed. As a quantum fissure increases in size, the risk of such catastrophic effects increases exponentially.

Aggravating factors that can increase the size and severity of a quantum fissure include chroniton particles, anti-time anomalies and concentrated subspace field pulses.

If you believe you might have passed through a quantum fissure into a parallel quantum universe, refer to section 4.15, "Determining if You Have Been Shifted into a Parallel Quantum Universe," for more information.

To seal a quantum fissure:

- Extend a low-intensity subspace field around it. Doing so will attract cosmic particles, which in turn will interact with spaceborne dust drawn into the fissure, rendering it visible.

- Determine if the quantum fissure was caused by a

starship or other warp-capable vessel by scanning the fissure for an ion trail. If one is detected, the energy signature present in the ionized particles will serve to identify the vessel that caused the rupture. This will enable you to use the correct vessel to reverse the damage.

- Scan the quantum fissure with a subspace differential pulse, using it to isolate a quantum reality that matches that of your RNA.

- Transmit a subspace message along the differential pulse back into your own reality. This is important because, even though you might perceive yourself to have been displaced from your original reality, a parallel version of you most likely is still in your original universe, along with whatever vessel you used to breach the quantum barrier. You will need to recover that vessel in order to return to your own reality and close the fissure.

- Pilot the vessel into the quantum fissure, and use the warp coils to emit a broad-spectrum inverse warp field at a power level of approximately 1.785 cochranes.

   This should be sufficient to seal the breach.

If you are successful in sealing the breach and returning to your home universe, you most likely will return to a point in time shortly prior to your original impact with the quantum fissure. However, temporal effects are highly unpredictable in this scenario, and the range of timeslip could prove substantial, depending upon a variety of specific factors.

1.16 DETECTING AND COUNTERACTING INVIDIUM CONTAMINATION

Invidium is a chemical compound that was widely used within the Federation during the late 22nd and early 23rd centuries. Its primary application was in medical stasis containers, although several secondary applications were known. Invidium's major drawback was that it interfered with sensitive electromagnetic systems, such as transporters, antigrav generators and magnetic field emitters. For this reason, the use of invidium was discontinued by the United Federation of Planets during the mid-23rd century. However, a few neighboring civilizations continue to use invidium, which makes the risk of invidium contamination of Federation vessels and facilities a remote but plausible risk.

A number of phenomena can serve as warning signs of possible invidium contamination. It is important to seek out these clues, because invidium does not register on standard internal scans. The most telling characteristic of invidium is that it will interact spontaneously with various forms of glass, resulting in random nucleosynthesis and substratum deformation of the molecular lattice. Other telltale signs will include sudden power fluctuations and systemic failure in such systems as antigrav palettes, transporter energizer and phase transition coils, comm relays, magnetic constrictors, phaser couplings, and a variety of other key systems. If invidium damages the plasma injectors of a warp nacelle assembly, it will result in an uneven flow of energized plasma to the warp coils, producing an unstable warp field that will tear apart a vessel moving at warp velocity.

It is important to note that invidium is unable to propagate unassisted. In most cases, it is spread by crew personnel who are unaware that their hands, uniforms, or tools are contaminated. As they move through the ship or station and perform routine tasks at various stations, they unknowingly promote the spread of contamination. If invidium is allowed to contaminate such key systems as warp reactors, matter-antimatter regulators, or the central computer core, it can rapidly cripple a vessel or station and lead to catastrophic failures that will ultimately result in destruction of the afflicted ship or facility.

Once invidium contamination has been confirmed and affected systems have been identified and isolated, invidium can be rendered inert by lowering its temperature to –200° Celsius. An effective and easily managed means to this end is gaseous cryonetrium, which is standard issue aboard Federation vessels and starbases as a plasma-fire suppressant. (Another less easily controlled but equally effective substance for neutralizing invidium is liquid nitrogen.)

Although rendering invidium inert will allow a contaminated starship to resume nominal operational status, a thorough decontamination will require an extended maintenance phase at a fully equipped starbase.

2.0

UNCONVENTIONAL MEDICINE

2.00   INTRODUCTION

Exploration into deep space often presents unique medical challenges and bizarre medical emergencies. Often, the medical dilemmas one encounters can be dealt with by extrapolating from known first-aid procedures or simply following the instructions provided by a medical tricorder's database.

Some situations, however, are not so predictable. Many of the scenarios detailed in this section are unique to particular planets or species, and might seem at first to be limited in their relevance. However, in such fields as exophysiology and emergency medicine aboard a starship, the difference between life and death often lies in one's ability to recognize parallels and make the cognitive leap from observation of the unknown to a reasonable diagnosis. Hopefully, the examples and information contained in this section will help you toward that goal should the need ever arise.

2.01   ANESTHETIZING HUMANOIDS WITH TRICORDER SIGNALS

In most humanoid species, certain similarities in brain-wave function have made possible the use of direct cortical anesthetic signals. Specifically, the propagation of harmonically shifted delta waves into humanoid brain tissue mimics the effects of chemical anesthesia used in less-advanced medical cultures, but it poses far fewer risks to the patient—most notably, it does not create the hazard of unexpected drug interactions, which in the case of newly encountered species might be exacerbated by unfamiliarity with the patient's physiology and biochemistry.

In a field medical emergency, it might become necessary

to perform surgery despite the lack of proper surgical equipment. An alternative technique that has been used successfully to anesthetize patients in these situations is to use a tricorder to induce in the patient's cerebral cortex brain-wave activity that resembles that of Stage 4 sleep. This is accomplished by using the tricorder to generate delta waves—which are characterized as long in wavelength, irregular in pattern, and slow in frequency—that will override the electrical impulses in the patient's brain, thereby resulting in a deep, dreamless state of unconsciousness that will persist until the delta waves generated by the tricorder are discontinued.

- Ascertain the correct delta wave signature to use when anesthetizing a patient. Activate the tricorder's BIO scan function, select Sense protocol E and isolate the patient's brain-wave signature with the F1 data key. Use the Library selector to choose the brain-wave activity sensor package from the medical submenu.

- If the patient is conscious, choose command key Alpha and use the Library selector to initiate a delta wave extrapolation. When the delta wave configuration has been identified, press command key Delta and use the Library selector to initiate the delta wave generation sequence.

- If the patient is unconscious, choose command key Alpha and use the Library selector to initiate a delta wave duplication. Then press command key Delta to maintain the patient's unconscious state.

While the patient is kept unconscious, it is important to monitor all vital signs as closely as possible. A proper Stage 4 sleep state should be indicated by reduced respiration, heart rate, and blood pressure, and a total absence of alpha wave brain activity. Any sudden changes in brain wave activity or vital signs might indicate that the patient is in danger of prematurely regaining consciousness, which will likely induce a potentially fatal state of shock. In such a scenario, it is important to cease whatever surgical procedure is in process, if at all possible, and attempt to remodulate the tricorder's delta wave signature in order to restore the patient to Stage 4 sleep.

It is important to note that some members of humanoid species that display strong telepathic skills (e.g., Vulcans, Ullians, and Betazoids, among others) sometimes prove highly resistant to externally generated delta waves, and might require an additional field of inverted alpha waves in order to negate their attempts to regain consciousness.

Restoring to consciousness a patient anesthetized in this manner is, in most cases, as simple as ceasing the generation of delta waves. Unlike chemical anesthetics, which can require hours to be purged from the body and often have significant side effects, delta wave anesthetic mimics the effects of restorative sleep. Barring surgical complications, most patients recover full consciousness within 30 to 120 minutes. During that time, the patient's vitals should continue to be monitored for any signs of postoperative trauma or other complications related to surgery.

2.02 MODIFYING A TYPE-1 OR TYPE-2 PHASER INTO A SCALPEL

When an away team or individual finds it necessary to perform emergency surgery in the field without the benefit of specialized surgical equipment, one of the most serious risks is that of infection caused by improperly sanitized surgical tools. One of the most crucial implements in any surgical procedure is an accurate and sterile scalpel. With some minor adjustments, standard-issue hand phasers can be repurposed as surgical cutting instruments.

Two components of the phaser must be modified in order to use it safely and efficiently as a scalpel: The beam control assembly and the prefire capacitor.

- Remove the protective casing from the phaser device.

- Adjust the beam control assembly master circuit to allow for a more tightly condensed beam that will converge to apex at a distance of approximately 5 centimeters from the emitter crystal. This will reduce the total length of the beam to a size appropriate for surgical use. If a different beam length is required, this setting can be adjusted during use.

- Next, access the safety interlock circuit of the prefire capacitor, which is located immediately behind the housing of the prefire chamber.

- Increase the capacitance value to maximum. This will help reduce the beam intensity to well below normal specifications, which will be essential to preserving beam control and stability during a surgical procedure. It also will reduce the feedback from the emitter crystal, making it safe to maintain a continuous beam for this procedure.

- Set the phaser to its lowest beam intensity and narrowest beam width. The device can now be used to make surgical grade incisions through most flesh and organic carapace. In addition, if a dermal regenerator is not available for closing surgical incisions, adjust the phaser to beam width 3 and beam intensity 2. In its surgical configuration, this will enable the phaser to be used as a cauterizing device for closing small incisions in most organic tissues. If larger, internal incisions need to be closed manually, the phaser can be set to intensity 1 and width 4 for sterilization purposes.

2.03 PROGRAMMING A HOLOGRAPHIC EMITTER TO ARTIFICIALLY RESPIRATE A HUMANOID WHOSE LUNGS HAVE BEEN DESTROYED

Holographic respiration is a highly unorthodox procedure intended to be employed only in the most dire of circumstances—specifically, in the event that a patient's lungs are entirely destroyed and there is no other means of enacting artificial respiration. A number of scenarios could result in such an occurrence; they range from catastrophic damage by directed energy attack or projectiles to any of several caustic or toxic chemical agents.

Although the concept of using a holographic emitter system to artificially respirate a patient might seem farfetched, it is in fact a fairly straightforward technique that takes advantage of the holographic systems' ability to precisely control fields of electromagnetic force. Most humanoid species' lungs operate on a strictly mechanical principle: To inhale, they increase in volume, expanding the chest cavity. That expansion lowers the pressure in the chest cavity below the outside air pressure. Air then flows in through the sinus airways (from high pressure to low pressure) and inflates the lungs. Constricting the lung volume increases its internal pressure, forcing waste gases out of the lungs, through the airways, and out of the body. This simple mechanical process is easily duplicated by careful modulation of holographic fields.

- Stabilize the patient's blood oxygen levels with a tri-ox compound delivered through a rapid infuser. This will help stave off brain damage and minimize injury to other tissues while the holographic respiration system is configured.

- Develop a working mechanical model of the pulmonary system. The most delicate part of this configuration is determining how the respiratory system connects with other major organs. When dealing with exotic or previously unknown species, a pre-existing bio scan of the patient's anatomy will offer the best starting point. If no bio scan is readily available, the relevant data can be extracted from transporter pattern logs, or, in the case of well-known species, simulated from known general parameters.

Once a mechanical model of the lung structure is prepared:

- Modulate the holographic field geometry and density to contain blood flow within the simulated organs while allowing oxygen to pass through porous holographic barriers in one direction, to oxygenate blood, and permitting carbon dioxide and other waste gases to pass through the barrier in another direction, to remove them from the blood stream. The exact specifications of this field geometry will vary based on the recommended blood-gas profile of each species. This porous field will serve to simulate the functions of bronchial passages in normal cardiopulmonary transfer.

Once the holographic respiratory model is configured:

- Restrain the patient with an isotropic field. This is crucial because in order to keep such a complex simulation perfectly aligned with the patient's internal structures—in particular, keeping the artificial alveoli in proper proximity to the pulmonary capillaries to effect blood-gas transfer—the computer will be unable to compensate for even the smallest movement by the subject. The patient must remain in the isotropic restraint until such time as artificial lungs can be implanted, or donor lungs transplanted, to replace the original, destroyed organs.

Holographic respiration was invented by a Starfleet Emergency Medical Hologram (EMH) aboard the *Starship Voyager* on Stardate 48532.4. A member of the Delta Quadrant species known as Talaxians on board the starship became the victim of an organ-stealing species known as the Vidiians, who stole his lungs.

The EMH, faced with a rapidly dying patient whose alien physiology made the likelihood of a successful biological transplant or artificial implant poor at best, extrapolated the solution of artificial respiration based upon the workings of his own program and its emitter system.

Despite the EMH's unfamiliarity with Talaxian anatomy, the holographic respiration system managed to keep the patient alive for more than 24 hours until such time as the Vidiians could be convinced to use their advanced medical technology to help graft a new donated lung into the Talaxian.

In the years since contact with *Voyager* made this technique known to Federation science, it has been incorporated into medical facilities and EMH programs throughout Starfleet, with remarkable success.

2.04 ERASURE OF HUMANOID SHORT- AND LONG-TERM MEMORIES

In many situations, requirements of mission security, the Prime Directive, or other tactical concerns can make it necessary to suppress or erase a subject's short- or long-term memory. This is an extremely dangerous procedure and should not be undertaken except in the most dire of circumstances.

In most humanoid species known to Federation science, memories are stored in the brain tissue in the form of neurochemical engrams. These engrams can be directly manipulated in three different ways, depending upon the desired result: They can be altered, suppressed, or destroyed.

Altering a memory engram is a complex process that involves submolecular manipulation of neurochemical enzymes, often transplanting them into an engram from outside, or transferring them between different engrams in the subject's brain. Transferring engrams is often more successful than implantation, although both techniques have been used successfully. The primary advantage of altering an engram rather than suppressing or destroying it is that, if successful, it is much more difficult to detect, because it leaves no chemical traces or temporal synaptic gaps. One disadvantage of alteration is that if it should become necessary to reverse the procedure, it can be difficult, and sometimes impossible, to restore the engrams to their original configurations.

Suppression of memory engrams involves binding a chemical suppression agent onto the synaptic transmitters that permit the brain to access the information stored in the engram. The precise chemical formula of an effective suppression agent will vary based on the species, and sometimes the blood type, of the patient. Suppression agents can be formulated to be short-term, long-term, or permanent, and are easily administered once a scan has identified specific regions to be targeted. The primary advantage of chemical suppression is that it leaves the original engrams intact, making the process reversible if it should become necessary to do so. Its most serious disadvantage is that many sophisticated measures of brain chemistry are capable of detecting the presence of a foreign substance in brain tissue.

The overt destruction of selected memory engrams is a very dangerous technique that should be used only in cases where permitting an individual to retain certain knowledge would lead to definite catastrophic results. When selectively eliminating engrams, great care must be taken that the correct ones are targeted, because once they are chemically disassembled, they are gone forever. Even small errors can leave an individual robbed of vital skills, such as language and key elements of personal identity.

Targeting selected engrams can be accomplished by means of a variety of brain-tissue scans. In most humanoid species, memory engrams are laid down in layers on cerebral tissue, with newer memory layers deposited on top of older ones. Consequently, newer memories will be closer to the surface than older memories.

Of equal importance is the fact that each species stores memories in different parts of their brain anatomy. (Refer to chapter 22 of the *Starfleet Medical Comparative Anatomy Reference, 5th Edition,* for more complete information on this subject.) It is important to know which parts of a subject's brain anatomy deal with sense memories, learned skills, and identity, as well as which areas are devoted to short-term and long-term memory storage. Of equal importance is understanding the role of memory triggers in each species; in humans, the olfactory sense is a powerful trigger, whereas in Deltans touch is the most powerful sensory mnemonic trigger.

In addition to erasing or suppressing memories, recent advances have made it possible to create large volumes of new memories through the directed application of bioelectric fields coupled with chemical catalysts that simulate the process of memory formation. In this manner it is possible to simulate years' worth of experiences, and even to craft entirely new identities. This can be a useful though drastic technique for protecting deep-cover intelligence operatives who might be subjected to intensive questioning or memory scans. However, it should be noted that serious side effects can occur if the original memory patterns are not fully suppressed; resulting conditions can include split-personality disorder, schizophrenia, dissociative personality syndrome, and Bendii Syndrome (in Vulcans).

Further information is classified.

2.05 PROTOCOLS FOR TEMPORARY IMPLANTATION OF A TRILL SYMBIONT INTO A NON-TRILL HOST

Trill symbionts are adapted for survival in only two environments: their native, subterranean nursery pools on the Trill homeworld and implanted within Trill humanoid hosts. Once a symbiont is fully bonded with its humanoid host, separation almost inevitably leads to rapid death for both host and symbiont. Although efforts to prolong the lives of separated hosts beyond more than a few hours have been unsuccessful, there has been anecdotal evidence to suggest that in the absence of a new Trill host or access to a nursery pool, a healthy Trill symbiont can be sustained for nearly 72 hours by implanting it temporarily into a non-Trill humanoid host.

This alternative is a valuable one, because Trill symbionts tend to survive less than three hours in current stasis units.

Prepare the new, temporary host:

- Inject the new host with 50 cc of metraprovoline in order to more closely simulate the hormonal and bio-chemical profile of Trill humanoids. This adjustment should be effective within less than an hour after injection.

As soon as bio functions cease in the current Trill host, remove the symbiont as follows:

- Make a straight incision into the torso, from just below the sternum to approximately two centimeters above the diaphragm. Use care to set the incision depth at less than .25 mm, so as not to risk harming the symbiont itself. Working through this incision,

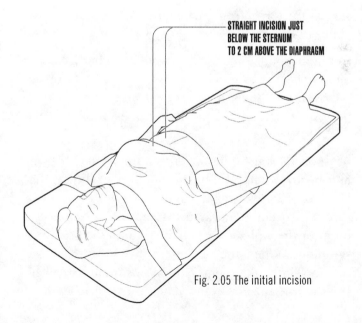

STRAIGHT INCISION JUST BELOW THE STERNUM TO 2 CM ABOVE THE DIAPHRAGM

Fig. 2.05 The initial incision

- Sever the symbiont's ganglial link to the host's spinal cord at a point slightly above the sacroiliac.

- Gently remove the symbiont from the host's body cavity.

Transfer the symbiont to the new host:

- Use a local anesthetic to prepare the incision area for the new, temporary host. It is important to use local, topical anesthetics and not general chemical anesthesia because the host must be conscious during the implantation procedure in order for the symbiont to establish a healthy bioneural link. Also, residual anesthetic chemicals in the host's bloodstream might prove harmful to the symbiont. (Regular Trill anesthetic formulas have proved incompatible with other humanoid species, and vice versa.)

- Once the new host is prepared, make a straight incision in the torso, from just below the sternum to just above the diaphragm.

- Gently introduce the symbiont into the body cavity; once it begins to enter the abdominal cavity of its own volition, allow it to proceed unassisted. It will position itself behind the lower intestine, near the base of the spine.

- As soon as the symbiont enters the non-Trill host and begins attempting to initiate a neural link, the host's blood pressure, pulse rate, and body temperature will become elevated. At this point, carefully monitor the alpha wave activity of both the host and symbiont. When they begin to synchronize, close the incision and administer a metabolic booster such as metrazene, coupled with a neurochemical isolator such as lethozine, to reduce the host's physiological response to the introduction of foreign tissue.

- If the host and symbiont's alpha wave patterns do not begin to synchronize after three minutes, abort the procedure immediately. Remove the symbiont from the temporary host body, close the incision, and administer hyronalin to reduce inflammation.

- Once the symbiont establishes a successful neural link with its temporary, non-Trill host, the next major complication will be tissue-rejection syndrome. Use an immunosuppressant agent to protect the symbiont from white blood cells in the host's body. Begin by administering the minimum amount needed to produce results, and increase the dosage gradually as the immune system becomes desensitized. Be careful, however, not to overdose the patient's system with immunosuppressants, or else you will risk damaging the patient's immune system permanently. As the duration of the implantation grows longer, likely side effects will include fever, dizziness, muscle fatigue, nausea, headache, dehydration, hyperacidity, and irregular heartbeat.

Removal of the symbiont from its temporary host:

- Make a straight incision as detailed above.
- Carefully sever the symbiont's ganglial bond to the spinal cord just above the sacroiliac.

Care of the temporary host after removal of the symbiont:

- Use a neurochemical isolator, such as lethozine, to alleviate possible symptoms of synaptic shock that the host might suffer as a result of the severed psychic bond.

- Purge the host's body of metraprovoline and stabilize its normal hormonal balance.

- Follow-up therapy normally includes antibiotics and hyronalin to reduce tissue inflammation.

It is important to note that the only anecdotal evidence currently available for this procedure details the implantation of a Trill symbiont into a human male. However, comparative baseline analysis indicates the procedure would be equally successful if carried out with a Bajoran, Deltan, Klingon, or Betazoid temporary host. However, it should be noted that Vulcans, Romulans, and Andorians have been determined to be unsuitable candidates as temporary hosts for Trill symbionts because their respective blood chemistries are not iron-based. (Vulcan and Romulan blood chemistry is copper-based; Andorian blood chemistry is cobalt-based.)

2.06   NEUTRALIZING DENEVAN NEURAL PARASITES

Denevan neural parasites (which are believed to have originated from outside the Milky Way Galaxy and are named for a Federation colony world they infested in 2267) are gelatinous, amoebalike life-forms analogous in structure to oversized brain cells. Colonies of parasites have exhibited behaviors consistent with a collective intelligence, and individual parasites are capable of limited, short-distance flight.

When the parasites make contact with humanoid life-forms, they attach themselves to the victim's back near the mid-spinal region and infiltrate the central nervous system with fibrous growths that quickly spread throughout the subject's body and brain. These tendrils allow the parasite to seize control of the victim's autonomic and higher functions and thereby control the subject's behavior. Victims who resist are subjected to intense, debilitating pain.

Denevan neural parasites are extremely virulent and reproduce at an alarming rate, which makes it possible for them to infest and control entire planetary populations in very brief periods, after which the parasites will compel the victims to aid in their transport across interstellar distances in order to infest other populations.

Denevan neural parasites are highly resistant to directed phaser fire and are able to withstand enormous physical damage before becoming incapacitated. Once they have infested a victim's central nervous system, pain-reducing medications and other sedatives will be rendered ineffective by the parasite, thereby making it nearly impossible to relieve patients' suffering while they are infested.

The only effective method of neutralizing Denevan neural parasites without causing permanent harm to humanoid victims is exposure to intense ultraviolet radiation. Early tests employed full-spectrum light radiation because the parasites were observed nesting only in deeply shaded areas; however, this was found to be unnecessary, as only the ultraviolet spectrum was shown to be effective in combatting the parasites.

Individual patients can be treated directly in most medical facilities or on board most starships; planetwide eradication of a large infestation of neural parasites will require an intense bombardment of UV radiation from satellite-based emitters. A UV exposure equivalent to five times the acceptable norm for a period of approximately 15 minutes will in most cases be sufficient to permanently neutralize the parasites.

Victims inside the bombardment zone will require post-procedural radiation treatment with hyronalin and other topical analgesics to alleviate epidermal damage and inflammation.

2.07   DETECTING AND REMOVING INTERPHASIC PARASITES

Interphasic (IP) parasites are a once-rare phenomenon believed to be indigenous to the planet Thanatos VII. Interphasic parasites have become increasingly common, however, following the introduction of interphasic fusion processes in the construction procedures at various industrial facilities throughout the Federation; consequently, the Starfleet Surgeon General and Starfleet Command have issued joint advisories about these dangerous organisms.

Interphasic parasites pose a grave risk to the health and survival of their humanoid hosts for two reasons. First, because of their nature as interphasic organisms, they are not normally detectable by tricorders or standard scanning protocols, despite their large size. Second, once they attach themselves to a humanoid host, they feed on the host's cellular peptides, quickly depleting them from the host. Unless the presence of interphasic parasites is suspected, the sudden disappearance of cellular peptides will likely continue without apparent explanation until the host's demise.

In addition to the serious medical risks posed by interphasic parasites, there are also potentially disastrous technological consequences to a shipboard infestation. IP parasites are attracted to a wide variety of shipboard operations, including those used in starship fabrication. Because interphasic parasites are drawn to plasma conduits and warp cores as breeding grounds, their presence in a starship's operational matrix can result in anything from severe disruptions of plasma flow in EPS taps and regulators, to catastrophic failures in warp core integrity.

The most straightforward means of detecting interphasic parasites is through the use of positronic scanners, which are capable of detecting the high-frequency interphasic energy pulses generated by interphasic parasites. Another method is to use an interphasic scanner to emit an interphasic neutralization field; this field will render objects of an interphasic nature visible to the naked eye.

Once the presence of IP parasites has been confirmed, it is fairly easy to neutralize them. An ultra-high-frequency interphasic pulse from a positronic generator will shift the organisms into a state of phasic dispersal, removing them far enough from the normal phasic state of matter to no longer pose a threat to humanoids or starship operations.

2.08   TREATMENT METHODS FOR AN OVERDOSE OF ANTI-INTOXICANTS

Despite efforts to curtail the use of anti-intoxicants without medical supervision, overdoses still occur, and they pose serious medical conundrums. Diagnosing an overdose of anti-intoxicants can be problematic, because victims often do not present with symptoms commonly associated with chemical overdoses. Most victims of AI overdose are rendered comatose, and display evidence of increased levels of foreign bacteria in the intestinal tract and bloodstream; this is because an AI overdose suppresses the body's autoimmune responses and interferes with synaptic chemical exchange. Unless anecdotal evidence suggests the use (and abuse) of anti-intoxicants, the condition is easily misdiagnosed—an error that commonly results in death for the victim.

Treatment of an AI overdose is equally challenging. Because anti-intoxicants are formulated to negate the active ingredients in most pharmaceuticals, ethanol variants, narcotics, and hallucinogens, it is extremely difficult to chemically purge an AI overdose.

To date, the most effective form of treatment has been found to be the simplest one.

Administer intravenous infusions of a 50-percent saline-diluted synthehol variant to which ethanol has been added at a ratio of one part per 10,000. (This formulation can be re-created in field-medical scenarios by mixing synthehol with ordinary, purified water and adding minute amounts of ethyl alcohol.) The diluted synthehol/ethanol will bond quickly with the anti-intoxicants in the bloodstream, making it possible for the patient's own body to excrete them normally. The infusion should be continued until the patient exhibits normal synaptic chemical exchange.

It is important to note that other drugs or large volumes of ethanol should not be used in place of synthehol; once the anti-intoxicant in the bloodstream is neutralized, there might be a brief delay in the return of normal synaptic exchange. In such cases, the rapid infusion would result in a standard chemical overdose, followed by severe shock and death. Synthehol, because it is easily neutralized by low volumes of natural adrenaline, poses far less risk to a patient.

HISTORICAL NOTE

A variety of social factors—most notably, recent cultural influences from such species as Klingons, Romulans, and Cardassians—have contributed to an increase in cases of a peculiar form of chemical overdose: the abuse of anti-intoxicants. Because of the prevalent use of ethanol-based beverages and other narcotics within several societies outside the Federation, many individuals have felt it necessary to partake of these dangerous controlled substances; however, in order to mitigate or neutralize those substances' effects, those same individuals have also adopted the use of dangerous levels of anti-intoxicant pharmaceuticals.

Anti-intoxicants were originally developed to counteract the deleterious and often life-threatening consequences of overdoses of such intoxicants as ethanol and various narcotics. By the mid-22nd century, anti-intoxicants became a staple of undercover law-enforcement and intelligence operatives, who used them as a preventative measure when scenarios involving the use of dangerous substances were considered both inevitable and necessary to the success of the operative's assignment.

The first confirmed incidence of an anti-intoxicant being used for recreational purposes occurred in 2293, and is believed to have been part of the inspiration for the Ferengi invention of synthehol.

2.09   PROVEN HERBAL REMEDIES FOR *MUGATO* VENOM

The *mugato* is an apelike creature found in a variety of habitats on Neural. A *mugato* has white fur; several large spines protruding from its back, and one spine on top of its head; large claws; and venomous fangs. The venom of a *mugato* is slow-acting (it can take a victim up to an hour to die), but extremely lethal. Multiple attempts to create a synthetic antivenom have failed. To date, the only known cure for *mugato* venom is found in a tuber indigenous to Neural, the *mahko* root.

- Obtain the *mahko* root.

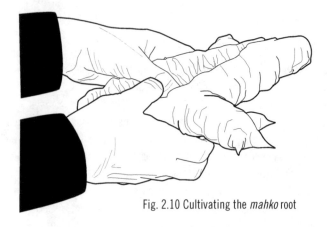

Fig. 2.10 Cultivating the *mahko* root

- Break the *mahko* root open laterally along its dorsal and ventral surfaces.

- Soften it by kneading with the hands.

- Firmly massage the root into the *mugato* bite wound.

- Make an incision on the palm of the hand of an unpoisoned individual (who must have iron-based hemoglobin), and

- Allow his or her blood to flow through the *mahko* root into the victim's wound.

The efficacy of this treatment rests in the complex natural compounds found in the *mahko* root. Iron-based blood that is allowed to flow into the root causes a chemical reaction with several of its natural compounds, producing a natural antivenom formula. The newly formed antivenom passes out of the root and enters the victim, where it quickly counteracts the symptoms of *mugato* poisoning and neutralizes the poison entirely within less than 24 hours. During this time, the patient will remain unconscious because of the natural antivenom's soporific side effects.

Research has revealed that the *Kahn-ut-tu* healers of Neural did not happen upon the *mahko* root's healing properties by accident. Although the *mugato* is normally a predator, zoological studies have confirmed that the *mahko* root is a staple of the diet of female *mugato* during periods of pregnancy and nursing.

2.10 NEGATING THE PSYCHOTROPIC EFFECTS OF OMICRON CETI III SPORES

Omicron Ceti III spores are the symbiotic extension of a plant-based, communally intelligent life-form that merges easily with animal hosts, including humanoids.

The spores provide certain beneficial effects to beings not indigenous to Omicron Ceti III—namely, they provide protection against the harmful effects of berthold radiation, which ordinarily is rapidly fatal to humanoids. In exchange for this benefit the spores form a symbiotic relationship with their hosts, who are enlisted to help spread and fertilize the spores.

This symbiosis subjugates the host's free will, resulting in a mental state that places the welfare of the spores and the plants that create them above all other concerns. Telltale signs of a symbiotically subjugated individual include unusually pronounced expressions of emotional contentment, a high degree of passivity, reduced inhibitions, and a near-total obsession with exposing other potential hosts to the spores.

These symptoms are related to the neurochemical bond between the spores and the hosts they inhabit. The spores appear to incite the body to produce an overabundance of serotonin (or similar neurochemicals) that block normal synaptic functions, rendering the subject susceptible to suggestion, in much the same manner as a hypnagogic state.

Neutralizing the spores' effect can be achieved with the application of sophisticated chemical counteragents delivered over a wide area in an aerosol form; however, in many cases such resources and methods will not be available.

The simplest way to counteract the spores' effect on a single subject is to provoke the individual to a state of extreme negative or aggressive emotion. This increases adrenaline levels and generates a number of neurochemical changes in the subject, including sharp reductions in serotonin. The reduction of serotonin leads to the polarization of neurons used by the symbiotic spores to establish and maintain connection with, and control over, a host's higher functions.

If it is necessary to produce an emotional response on a large scale—for instance, the entire population of a small colony—ultrasonic signals have been shown to be very effective at inducing extreme anger and agitation in most humanoid species. Another viable method would be to use wide-area, low-level phaser blasts from orbit, at power levels too low to cause unconsciousness but high enough to produce severe discomfort.

Despite the spores' official nomenclature, recent reports have indicated that the spores have been successfully smuggled off Omicron Ceti II and imported onto worlds afflicted by berthold radiation by colonists wishing to stake claims on otherwise inhospitable land. The spores have been detected as uninvited imports on planets as far away as Yridia, and even in the Gamma Quadrant. Consequently, their detection and rapid neutralization is to be considered a priority wherever they are detected.

2.11 DIAGNOSING AND COUNTERACTING VARIANTS OF THE PSI 2000 VIRUS

The original Psi 2000 virus is a water-based disease organism originally encountered by the crew of the *Starship Enterprise* in 2266. The virus is created by a variety of factors, one of which is the presence of high- or variable-gravity environments, such as those encountered in close orbit over unstable stars or erratic binary pairs. The virus is transmitted through contact with perspiration or other bodily fluids of an infected individual.

Its primary symptoms are sweating and a marked reduction of inhibition similar to that of alcohol intoxication. The virus reacts in the bloodstream in a manner similar to that of alcohol, interfering with the blood's capacity to carry oxygen. This causes rapid vasodilation and sharply increased pressure on cerebral tissues, resulting in erratic behavior and impaired motor function. The body's immune-system response, which alone is incapable of neutralizing the virus, is a quickly rising fever that produces heavy perspiration and promotes the spread of the virus.

Other variants on the Psi 2000 virus have been detected; in 2364, one such variant claimed the lives of the crew of the *U.S.S. Tsiolkovsky* and infected the crew of the *U.S.S. Enterprise*-D. This variant did not respond to the same counteragents that neutralized the first Psi 2000 virus, and required the application of a more broad-based treatment.

The current standard protocol for counteracting a Psi 2000 virus is an injection of anti-intoxicant infused with a tailored retrovirus that will dismantle the specific viral strain. Two broad-based Psi 2000 counterviruses are currently on file in the standard Starfleet Medical Database, and the SMD includes an appendix with a formula for extrapolating the countervirus formula to other, as-yet-unknown strains of the virus.

It is important to note that the standard regimen of antiviral agents used against most other infectious pathogens will in most cases be ineffective against a Psi 2000 virus because of its peculiar bonding properties; because of the specific manner in which this organism attaches itself to blood cells, an incorrect treatment regimen, if pursued aggressively, could result in the inadvertent suffocation of the patient.

2.12   RECOGNIZING AND TREATING SYMPTOMS OF TEMPORAL NARCOSIS

Prolonged exposure of a humanoid to a temporally disrupted environment, even when the subject is protected by a low-power subspace force field, can lead to the rapid onset of temporal narcosis. The warning signs of temporal narcosis include impaired judgment, irrational behavior, dizziness, loss of balance and motor skills, and eventually panic.

If you have a subject who exhibits symptoms of temporal narcosis:

- Remove the patient to a temporally stable area as soon as possible. Determine whether the patient is experiencing any signs of shock or continued temporal disorientation. If so, it might be necessary to sedate the patient before continuing.

- Next, neutralize any molecular phase imbalance in the subject by exposing him or her to a low-power antichroniton field. During this process, pay special attention to synaptic chemistry and neuroelectric patterns. Prolonged irregular patterns or excessively regimented and identical patterns can both be indicators of temporal disruption at the synaptic level; if this is the case, specifically modulated microbursts of directed antichronitons will need to be administered in a controlled environment in order to reverse the effects of temporal narcosis. (Fortunately, this level of disruption is rare, and usually occurs only after extremely long periods of exposure in temporally disturbed environments.)

FIELD EMERGENCIES INVOLVING TEMPORAL NARCOSIS

It is possible to generate a low-level antichroniton field with standard field equipment.

- Reconfigure a combadge's subspace transceiver assembly to emit a low-power unmodulated subspatial disruption field.

- Use a tricorder to focus a narrow tachyon scanning burst into the subspatial disruption.

The result will be a low-power antichroniton field emission.

As little as 30 seconds' exposure to this seemingly ad hoc treatment should be enough to stabilize most victims of temporal narcosis for up to 24 hours, which in most cases should be long enough to reach medical help.

3.0

DANGEROUS LIFE-FORMS

3.00   INTRODUCTION

Within and outside the Federation are more animal and sentient life-forms than can possibly be detailed in one reference work. Many are relatively benign in their interactions with humanoids, but many are hostile and extremely violent.

Although the standard-issue *Starfleet Basic Survival Manual* includes protocols for avoiding or discouraging most terrestrial and aquatic predators, and for evading sentient species known to be aggressively antagonistic, certain scenarios and species warrant special, detailed discussion here.

3.01   HOW TO DRIVE OFF NONCORPOREAL EMOTIONAL PARASITES

Noncorporeal emotional parasites, or NCEPs, are a particular subgenus of plasma- and energy-based life-forms that have been encountered in a wide variety of locations throughout explored space. They appear to subsist on, and draw strength from, the bioelectric fields generated by humanoid brains as a by-product of certain heightened emotional states. Different species of NCEPs have shown a preference for different emotions, but there have been noted similarities.

If you believe an NCEP may have infiltrated your ship or facility, look for combinations of various warning signs:

- Stay alert to unusual emotional preoccupations becoming shared by groups of people, who individually and collectively have begun to assert an irrational mentality;

- Be wary of a single individual who becomes the focus of, or linking factor between, various mysterious events when that individual consistently lacks any recollection of the events and has no previous history of mental illness or memory loss;

- Pay particular attention to suddenly emerging, extremely intense group emotional states that persist for an unnaturally long duration. Powerful emotions such as rage, fear, lust, or euphoria tend to be short-lasting in most humanoid species; when they seem to become prolonged and shared by many individuals, this is often a warning of an NCEP's influence.

Once you become aware of an NCEP's presence and interference with one or more members of your crew, the next step is to analyze its form and behavior and seek out its weaknesses.

Key inquiries include:

- Is the NCEP visible? Some manifest as cohesive gatherings of charged plasma that will luminesce more brightly as the creature gains strength; this can be useful when gauging the effectiveness of countermeasures.

- What emotional responses strengthen it? Does it respond to more than one emotion?

- If a given emotion is found to strengthen it, does the opposite emotion weaken it? Is it vulnerable to a variety of emotional states?

- If reversal of emotional responses does not weaken it, can it be confused or driven off through the application of logical paradoxes? Can it be contained in systems configured to store and transfer energy, such as a main computer or an EPS router?

Different Types of NCEPs

Although some NCEPs, such as the Laughing Sprite of Peloris Minor or the "Passion Poltergeist" of Galvan Prime, seem relatively benign and have proved easy to dispel by conscious efforts at resistance, others have shown themselves to be far more dangerous and, in some cases, lethal. Two such entities were encountered by the *Starship Enterprise* during its missions of exploration under the command of Captain James T. Kirk.

In 2267, the crew of the *Enterprise* encountered an NCEP that fed off the emotion of terror in humanoids. It managed to commit several grisly murders on the planet Argelius II for which *Enterprise* chief engineer Montgomery Scott was charged and subsequently acquitted. The entity, known by many names in a variety of star systems, was dubbed Redjac by the crew of the *Enterprise*. When the entity took refuge in the ship's computer, the crew was able to expel it by forcing that computer to execute a series of impossible and paradoxical calculations.

The following year, the *Enterprise* was invaded by the Beta XII-A entity, which thrived on emotions of hatred and anger. It compelled the crew of the *Enterprise* and the captured crew of a Klingon battle cruiser to wage a self-perpetuating conflict. The Beta XII-A entity displayed remarkable abilities to shape and affect matter, transforming energy weapons into swords and knives and healing wounded Starfleet crewmen and Klingons so that they could resume their hostilities. The entity even proved capable of fabricating memories in certain crew members, falsifying motivations for their rage and hatred. Ultimately, the Klingon and Starfleet crews united in laughter to drive the entity away.

DO NOT CONFRONT AN NCEP ALONE. This is one of the most important tactical issues to keep in mind when dealing with an NCEP. Most NCEPs have immense power reserves and are more than a match for most individual, organic minds.

Organize large groups of people. Use whatever means necessary to form a coalition to oppose the NCEP. If you are seeking to deprive it of strength and weaken it through emotional counterattack, the more minds you can turn to the effort the better.

Deprive it of what it needs. Regardless of whether opposing emotional states weaken the NCEP, it is crucial that the crew cease "feeding" it by indulging in its emotion of choice. Until its source of sustenance is cut off, it will be all but impossible to force it away.

3.02   AVOIDING MIND CONTROL BY ELASIAN WOMEN

Elasian women possess glands near their tear ducts that secrete a pheromone with mild psychotropic properties. The pheromone is released in their tears, and can be readily absorbed through skin—or ingested. Because of the powerful nature of the pheromone, male humanoids are often compelled to touch the tears, which then take full effect.

The chief effect of female Elasian tears on a humanoid male is to render him affectionate, submissive, and easily controlled by the female with whose tears he has come into contact. The effects of female Elasian tears on non-Elasian males have been shown in most cases to be temporary; if a subject is aware of the attempts to control him, the effects can be negated relatively quickly—if he has a greater love or passion for someone, or something, else.

If you suspect that a member of your crew has been placed under control by an Elasian female and is unaware of his situation, look for him to exhibit certain signs:

- Servile behavior toward a specific Elasian woman.

- An unusually soft and placating tone of voice toward an Elasian woman.

- Sudden loss of interest in other relationships, duties and activities.

In order to break the effects of the psychotropic pheromone, it will be necessary to follow a few simple steps:

- Separate the subject from the Elasian female. Do so tactfully, and not by force.

- Do not, under any circumstances, use any kind of force or restraint on the Elasian who is controlling the subject; he will respond violently to defend her, and might pose a serious threat to his own safety and that of others.

- Use psychological counseling to refocus the subject's thoughts on other people or things he finds important. This is the safest means of breaking the effects of Elasian mind control, though there are pharmacological options.

- If you choose to break the Elasian mind control chemically, inject the subject with a mild dose of lethozine mixed with antosterone (a multispecies pheromonal inhibitor).

Notes of Interest

Coordinated medical, historical, and anthropological research into the history of the Elasian species suggests that the mind-controlling properties of female Elasian tears arose as an evolutionary response to the threat of male violence. Studies suggest that until 3,200 years ago Elasian society was dominated by a violent, patriarchal ruling caste. Then a rapid shift to matriarchal forms of government spread across the Elasian homeworld within a few hundred years, during a time period in which Elasian mitochondrial DNA reveals the first appearance of a dominant new gene: the one that creates the psychotropic pheromone in Elasian women's tears.

Although the effects of the tears on non-Elasian males have been shown in most cases to be temporary, the tears affect Elasian men like a tailored retrovirus, altering their DNA and imprinting changes on the subjects' Y chromosomes. Consequently, once imprinted by an Elasian female, an Elasian male, and all his male progeny, become docile and subservient to the imprinting female and all her female offspring in perpetuity.

3.03   SURVIVING ATTACK BY A CRYSTALLINE ENTITY

The Crystalline Entity was a silicon-based spaceborne life-form capable of faster-than-light interstellar travel. It has been described as resembling a "giant snowflake" measuring several hundred meters in diameter and more than 2 kilometers in overall length.

The first recorded encounter with a Crystalline Entity by Federation citizens occurred at the Omicron Theta science colony in 2336. The entity laid waste to all organic matter on the planet surface. The creature attacked any world with organic matter and rich surface resources, which it consumed and converted into pure energy. In this manner the entity obliterated entire planets. It proved equally dangerous to spacegoing vessels.

Although only this one Crystalline Entity has so far been encountered, exobiology specialists both within and outside the Federation speculate that there might be others in as yet unexplored regions of the galaxy.

- If you encounter a Crystalline Entity, notify Starfleet and the appropriate local authorities IMMEDIATELY.

    Before the last reported Crystalline Entity was destroyed, a Starfleet crew successfully initiated two-way contact with the creature; earlier reports, coupled with sensor evidence from that encounter, indicate that Crystalline Entities are highly intelligent. Therefore:

- If a Crystalline Entity is encountered, the standing directive for all Federation vessels is to attempt peaceful contact through the use of a graviton beam modulated with low-power, low-frequency pulses in standard hailing patterns.

- If attempts at peaceful communication fail—or are not possible for whatever reason—the most prudent course of action is to avoid an encounter or flee from it quickly. If you are aboard a warp-capable vessel, set course at maximum velocity away from populated worlds and reinforce your shields to their highest capacity. The Crystalline Entity should tire of pursuit after only a short time.

- If you are on a planet surface in an exposed area when the Crystalline Entity is detected, the safest destination is underground. In particular, seek deep caves located below—or laced heavily with—deposits of fistrium, kelbonite, or similarly refractive compounds. The Crystalline Entity consumes organic matter by sweeping the surface with an accelerator beam that is unable to penetrate super-dense refractive metals.

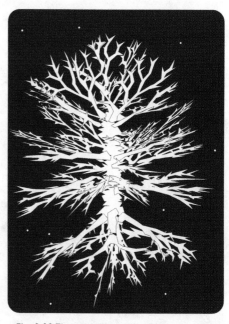

- If you are in an urban area on a Federation world, seek refuge in an up-to-date defensive shelter, particularly one that is shielded against high-energy scans. Most Federation defense installations have at least one such deep

Fig. 3.03 The crystalline entity. Contact Starfleet immediately upon recognition!

shelter area. If access to such a facility is unavailable, a general rule of thumb is that the deeper below the surface you travel, the more protection you will have from the Crystalline Entity's attack.

- Finally, if retreat or refuge is impossible and attempts at communication fail or result in further hostility, your last option is to defend yourself. The same kind of modulated graviton beam that is used to communicate with the Crystalline Entity can be used to inflict damage upon it. Once the graviton beam is locked on, increase its resonant harmonics in order to create a feedback loop that will fracture the Crystalline Entity's structural lattice.

Although it is possible to destroy the entity by increasing the resonant harmonic frequency to maximum, current engagement protocols call for a more restrained response. An appropriate show of force should be enough to convince the entity to retreat. Only if this measure fails, should deadly force be employed. Follow standard Starfleet guidelines at all times.

3.04   DEALING WITH "OMNIPOTENT" BEINGS

Since the earliest days of interstellar exploration, starship crews have reported encounters with beings that described themselves as "omnipotent." Some of these beings have consistently presented themselves in corporeal form (e.g., The Q Continuum, Trelane, the Douwd) while others have manifested in some combination of pure energy and matter (e.g., the Organians, the Metrons). In most cases they have demonstrated a remarkable ability to control energy and matter at a nuclear level, seemingly at will. The Q have also proved they are capable of influencing temporal effects and resolving or reconciling apparent paradoxes.

The most important caveat to keep in mind when encountering a so-called omnipotent being is to remain calm. Some, such as the Q or Trelane, behave much like bullies. Others, such as the Metrons or Organians, take a more patronizing tone toward corporeal species but are generally pacifist and benevolent of intention. The Douwd generally divorce themselves from the affairs of other species and are typically pacifist, but they can be very dangerous if antagonized (one Douwd single-handedly erased the Husnock species from existence in an instant of rage).

In many cases, these powerful beings will seek to engage you or your crew in manufactured competitions, trials, or other biased tests. Although you should humor their requests to a point (and preserve a sense of humor when dealing with them), their actions should not be encouraged. Do not be goaded by their taunts or threats; in most cases, a diplomatic and passive refusal to cooperate should be enough to extricate you from such an encounter.

If a self-described omnipotent being places you in a position where refusal to interact on its terms might lead to violent reprisal, the next approved course of action is cautious negotiation. Seek the minimum degree of participation required to fulfill the being's interest, and attempt to barter a mutually agreeable set of terms that will not require you to violate Starfleet directives or cause harm to yourself, your crew, or outside parties.

In order to facilitate your negotiation, solicit information from the being about its species, desires, and goals. The Federation currently maintains a standing directive to amass accurate data on such species for the joint purposes of pure research and self-defense. Past encounters have indicated that the most successful means of obtaining such intelligence is to play on the ego of the being by making it the center of attention.

If an encounter with one of these beings (or a similar intelligence) degenerates into a situation that might result in casualties or fatalities, do not be afraid to abandon personal or organizational pride in the interest of saving lives. Do not hesitate to ask the omnipotent being for mercy, help, or rescue—again, such requests often bolster the ego, making them more likely to behave in a nonthreatening manner.

The watchword for these types of encounters is "patience." Be careful in your choice of words when communicating with such beings, particularly the Q. Most available evidence suggests that many of these beings, because of their nearly immortal lifespans, are often lonely, bored, and simply desirous of stimulating interaction. Regardless of the nature of your interaction with such a being, all such encounters—both by Starfleet personnel and Federation civilians—should be reported immediately to Starfleet Command.

3.05 PROTOCOLS FOR NANITE INFESTATION OF COMPUTERS

Nanites are microscopic machines, constructed at the nuclear level, that are used for various medical and engineering applications. Each nanite possesses several gigabytes of operating memory and is capable of entering living cells or active machinery to effect repairs or upgrades at the molecular level. They are capable of automated self-replication, independently learning new functions, and interacting in a synaptic fashion. Consequently, a sufficiently large group of nanites working in concert can, under

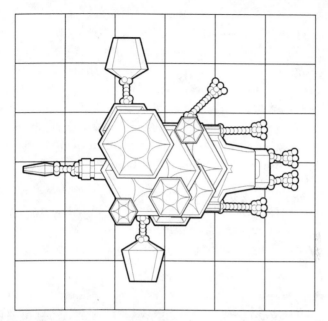

Fig. 3.05a Example of a nanite

the right circumstances, achieve a sentient level of group consciousness.

An incident aboard the *U.S.S. Enterprise* NCC-1701-D in 2369, however, demonstrated the danger posed by improperly monitored nanite colonies. Because most nanites are drawn to energy sources and sources of raw materials for self-replication, a rogue colony of nanites will gravitate toward the high-energy subspace field generators in a faster-than-light computer core. As their numbers increase, they ingest and reorder large quantities of silicon, carbon nanotubes, and other critical elements used in the construction of isolinear matrices.

- Early warning signs of potential nanite infestation of a computer network can include major operating failures cascading through various, otherwise unrelated systems. These errors, unlike the types of isolated, brief errors caused by power surges and software viruses, will be prolonged and unrecognized by the computer itself. The errors will become more frequent, widespread, and serious as the infestation grows and spreads. Physical evidence of nanite infestation will take the form of submolecular striations, disintegration and overall degradation of integrity in the computer core's linear crystal matrices.

- Once a nanite infestation has been detected, ascertain whether the nanite colony has attained sentience. Various methods of contact offer possible avenues of interaction, including standard hailing protocols.

- If the nanite group is determined to be nonsentient, they should be neutralized. Expose them to a low-level gamma burst, which will render them inert without destroying them. They can then be purged from the isolinear matrices through the use of a magnetic resonance wave. If the nanites prove resistant to the low-energy gamma burst, they can be destroyed by exposing them to a high-energy gamma burst. Neither type of gamma exposure will pose any risk to the isolinear chips or their data content.

- If the nanite colony is determined to be sentient:

  ▲ Attempt communication in accordance with standard Federation protocols. Nanites operating in this collective manner are able to evolve new functions, such as language skills, at a highly accelerated rate, and they should be able to interface with the universal translator program to establish fluent interaction within a short time after achieving sentience. Under no circumstances should you resort to violence;

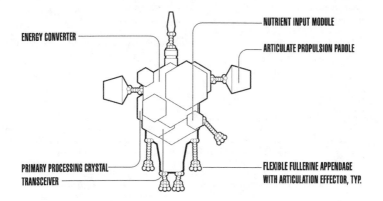

ENERGY CONVERTER

NUTRIENT INPUT MODULE

ARTICULATE PROPULSION PADDLE

PRIMARY PROCESSING CRYSTAL TRANSCEIVER

FLEXIBLE FULLERINE APPENDAGE WITH ARTICULATION EFFECTOR, TYP.

Fig. 3.05b Workings of a nanite

nanites are highly adaptable, and if they are in your computer, they will learn to use the systems it controls to defend themselves.

▲ Once peaceful contact with the nanite colony is established, the nature of their relationship to you, your computer, and the universe at large should be made clear immediately. If they are asked properly, the nanites are capable of repairing almost all damage they might have inflicted on your computer systems.

▲ After your computer is restored, your chief objective should be to seek the nanites' informed consent to relocate them out of your computer. They can be removed safely through the use of a low-power magnetic resonance wave.

Under the terms of a 2369 directive by the Federation Council, nanites that have achieved sentience are to be brought to Kavis Alpha IV, which has been designated as the official homeworld of evolved nanites. Although the nanite colonies there are currently maintaining an isolationist policy toward off-worlders, the Federation Council continues to hope that Kavis Alpha IV will one day become a member world of the United Federation of Planets.

3.06   NAVIGATING INSIDE A BORG CUBE OR SPHERE

Although the Federation's policy toward encounters with the Borg continues to be one of avoidance at all costs, in certain exceptional circumstances you or a member of your crew might find it necessary to enter a Borg sphere or cube vessel. If such a mission is absolutely necessary, there are certain protocols that, if faithfully observed, will maximize the chances of successfully finding one's way into and out of the vessels, which are notoriously confusing because of their repetitive interior layout and absence of distinguishing features.

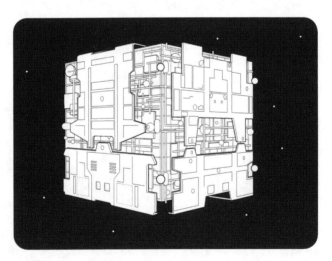

Fig. 3.06a Example of a Borg cube

Fig. 3.06b Example of a Borg sphere

Borg vessels of cubic or spherical design are generally highly symmetrical in their interior design. They are built outward from the core in a fractal pattern—i.e., one whose larger form emulates the smaller forms of which it is composed. Located in the core of each major Borg vessel is a singular device known as a vinculum. The vinculum is the primary node aboard each ship that connects its drones to the Borg collective mind and to the various systems and subsystems of each individual vessel.

- Follow a regular pattern, such as taking every second available right turn followed by every second available left turn, or some equally memorable variant.

- Do not vary from your pattern once it has been established; it is very easy to become disoriented inside a Borg ship once all points of reference to the outer hull or core are no longer visible.

- Do not try to leave position beacons at points inside

the vessel; the Borg ship will likely detect and either absorb or destroy them soon after they are deployed. Your best indicator of your position relative to the vessel's outer hull will be the strength of subspace signals received by your tricorder or communicator from outside the Borg vessel.

- If or when you need to retrace your path to return to your starting point, simply turn around and follow the reverse of your original pattern.

- Do not attempt to mark your path by leaving objects, flares, markers, or damage to the interior of the Borg ship. Borg vessels self-repair and will quickly obliterate or absorb foreign objects and "heal" damaged systems and surfaces.

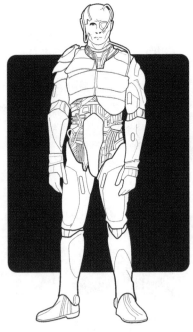

Likewise, do not attempt to use particular objects or intersections within the Borg vessel as reference points. Each Borg ship contains multiple identical intersections, consoles, and devices because of the fractal nature of their construction.

- Do not be overly concerned about encountering drones when you first enter. In many cases, Borg drones will

Fig. 3.06c Example of a Borg drone

ignore you unless the collective believes you pose an immediate and serious threat to the survival of the ship or the completion of its assignment.

- If you are attacked by the drones, retreat immediately and head toward open spaces. Try to avoid dead ends or extremely long, narrow passages lacking intersections.

- Above all, do not attempt to hide aboard a Borg ship. The various systems and internal sensors of a Borg vessel are all linked to the ship's drones and to the Borg collective at large. The longer you remain in one place, the greater the likelihood that you will be detected. Furthermore, a Borg ship can be directed by the hive mind to spontaneously generate new interior walls, close passages, and fill-in entire areas. Hiding aboard a Borg ship is therefore tantamount to surrender.

Keep in mind that the drones' defenses will adapt to your weapons and tactics very quickly. Alter your weapons' phase variance and nutation randomly and often, and fire sparingly; the

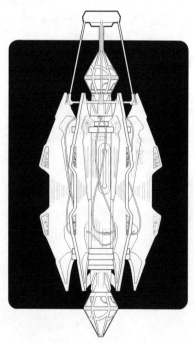

Fig. 3.06d Example of a Borg vinculum

less exposure the Borg have to your weapons, the less information they have to guide their adaptation sub-routines.

- If you incur hostile response by the drones aboard the Borg ship and are unable to escape in a timely fashion, attempt to disrupt the hive mind to increase confusion and increase your chances of escape.

  ▲ One method is to gain access to the collective's lower-priority command subroutines and initiate a shipwide sleep and regeneration cycle.

  ▲ If you have access to the ship's vinculum, inflicting serious damage to it will not only disrupt the drones aboard the ship, it will also sever their connection to the Borg collective and impair their ability to direct shipboard damage control.

3.07 RECOGNIZING AND NEUTRALIZING A DIKIRONIUM CLOUD CREATURE

Dikironium cloud creatures are extremely dangerous—and, fortunately, also very rare. They are very difficult to detect because they camouflage themselves by moving in and out of timephase at will. When shifted out of timephase, the creature is all but undetectable to sensors. Dikironium cloud creatures are naturally capable of traversing interstellar space.

When one does manifest in the same timephase as normal matter, it appears as a pale red, gaseous cloud and emits a distinctive, sickly sweet odor, like that of rotting flowers. The cloud moves of its own accord, and in total silence. Dikironium cloud creatures must take this form in order to feed.

The chief hazard posed by a dikironium cloud creature is that it will prey upon all organisms with iron-based serotypes. In its gaseous form it envelops its prey and penetrates the victim's body, then consumes all the victim's red blood cells. The dikironium cloud creature is an extremely efficient killer, capable of draining a healthy adult humanoid of red blood cells within a few seconds.

Compounding the danger posed by the creature is its innate resistance to attack. Its gaseous form is not combustible, and it is impervious to attack by projectile weapons, electric discharges, and phasers. Consequently, the best defense against a dikironium cloud creature is retreat.

If even a single dikironium cloud creature were to reach a populated world, the death toll could easily exceed one million victims in less than a month. Because dikironium cloud creatures have demonstrated no signs of sentient intelligence and have proved themselves unremittingly hostile and dangerous to a wide variety of humanoid species, the standing protocol if a dikironium cloud creature is encountered is to destroy it. The only method so far proven effective is a low-yield antimatter detonation at point-blank range while the creature is in normal space-timephase.

Set a trap as follows:

- To lure the creature into the necessary proximity of the bomb, place a quantity of several liters of iron-based blood in a sealed container. Transport it to the creature's last known location along with the low-yield antimatter explosive.

- Arm the bomb and set it to be triggered by remote command.

- Activate a remote nanotransmitter, to be left behind to permit you to monitor the trap area.

- Open the container of blood and transport yourself to a safe distance—preferably, a ship in orbit. Note that, if possible, this task should be performed by a crew member of a species that does not have iron-based blood—for instance, a Vulcan (copper-based hemoglobin) or Andorian (cobalt-based serotypes).

- As soon as the dikironium cloud creature shifts into normal timephase within any range up to 20 meters of the device, trigger the explosion. The subspace compression wave caused by an antimatter explosion will prevent the dikironium cloud creature from shifting its timephase to escape.

A CAUTIONARY EXAMPLE

Before you confront a dikironium cloud creature, consider this account of the species' first encounter with Starfleet: In 2257, the crew of the *Starship Farragut*, commanded by Captain Garrovick, discovered a dikironium cloud creature on planet Tycho IV. In the span of a single encounter, the creature killed 200 members of the *Farragut's* crew, including Captain Garrovick. One survivor of the battle against the creature was Lieutenant James T. Kirk, who returned to Tycho IV eleven years later as the captain of the *Starship Enterprise*. The creature claimed two more lives before Kirk finally destroyed it with an antimatter detonation.

If you are acting alone and are unable to produce or obtain a sufficient volume of fresh blood to lure the dikironium cloud creature, do not use yourself as bait. In such a circumstance, retreat and signal for help before taking action.

Remember, a dikironium cloud creature can strike from any direction, in silence and with great speed, and kills almost instantly. If you use yourself as bait, you will most likely be killed before you can trigger the detonator.

3.08 FENDING OFF AN ATTACKING *MUGATO*

A *mugato* is an apelike creature native to Neural that has white fur, poisonous fangs, a single large horn on the top of its head, and spiny protrusions along the length of its back. The *mugato* is an omnivorous predator that will not hesitate to attack humanoids or creatures larger than itself. It is extremely territorial and generally a solitary creature, except during its mating season.

The best policy for dealing with *mugato* is to avoid them at all costs. When on Neural or other worlds known to harbor *mugato* populations (which spread to several worlds within and beyond the Federation due to poaching enterprises gone awry), reduce or eliminate food odors and personal scents from yourself, your garments, your campsite, and your vehicles. Futhermore, do not sleep in the same clothes you wear while cooking. Store soiled clothes in a manner that will inhibit detection of their odors. Do not store food in open areas. Do not allow refuse, personal waste or other odor-producing materials to build up in or near your encampment. Following these simple procedures will reduce the likelihood of an encounter with a foraging or hunting *mugato*.

Fig. 3.08 A *mugato*

When you are traveling in the dusty, rocky

hills in which mugato prefer to hunt, be alert for signs of its presence. Such signs can include, but are not limited to: pawprints; spoor; tufts of its white, coarse fur left on brambles or other thorny growth; and partially consumed masses of *mahko* root, which female *mugato* consume when pregnant or nursing.

If you encounter a *mugato,* proceed cautiously. If you see the creature before it sees you:

- Freeze. Remain motionless and quiet. Do not do anything to draw the creature's attention.

- If it looks away or begins to move off, cautiously back away along the path you came.

- Get to cover before the *mugato* sees you.

- Stay downwind of the creature, if possible.

- Don't leave any of your own blood, excrement, clothing, or food in the *mugato*'s territory. If it discovers them, it will use the scent information to track you back to your camp.

If the *mugato* sees you from a distance, run. Attempt to use the local terrain to block the creature's line of sight to you, then take cover. Do not attempt to flee to high ground; *mugato* are excellent climbers and will overtake you easily. If there is no chance of reaching cover, try to reach deep, moving water. Wild *mugato* are unable to swim.

If you are unable to escape a pursuing *mugato,* or if it attacks you by surprise:

- Defend your head and throat at all costs. The *mugato* prefers to tear out the throats of its prey.

- If you are unarmed, strike at the creature's eyes, ears, and genitals; they are its most vulnerable points.

- If you have a pointed weapon of a length greater than 23 cm, such as a dagger—or even a sharpened stick—aim for the underside of its jaw, at a point just behind the chin. This is a soft spot in the creature's anatomy, and a properly targeted attack here can puncture the creature's brainpan, killing it instantly. Even a less-than-perfect wound here can sever the creature's jaw tendons, rendering it unable to deliver its highly venomous bite.

- Do not attempt to strike at the creature's lower torso. Its thick fur will absorb most blunt attacks, and its body is heavily muscled.

MUGATO FACTS

- Each *mugato* defends an area of "personal space" (which can vary from a few dozen square meters to several kilometers) and encroaching on that space can provoke an attack.

- *Mugato* are very strong and very fast. They can run almost as quickly as a Terran horse or Klingon *sark*. Most humanoids cannot outrun them.

- *Mugato* have superior auditory, visual, and olfactory senses.

- *Mugato* are excellent climbers and can easily pursue prey into trees and up steep rocky inclines.

- *Mugato* aggressively defend food, whether it is their kill or a carcass they have scavenged. Avoid carrion, even if no *mugato* presence is evident.

- Pregnant and nursing female *mugato* on Neural consume large quantities of natural *mahko* root. If you encounter large patches of this plant, leave the area immediately, as it will likely be central to a *mugato* nesting area.

- Do not attempt to pierce the creature's chest wall. Its ribs are very close together and connected by thick, extremely resilient cartilage. Likewise, its sternum is very thick—three times thicker than that of an average human male—and will repel most stabbing attacks.

3.09   WRESTLING FREE OF A DENEBIAN SLIME DEVIL

The Denebian slime devil is one of the most dangerous and ubiquitous predators in the Alpha Quadrant. It is an amphibious animal life-form that hunts using a form of natural radar, and its forklike foreclaws are capable of tearing easily through such heavy garments as cold-weather jackets and standard-issue EVA suits. A fully grown adult of the species can be up to three meters long and can weigh up to 215 kilograms.

Although the preferred prey of the Denebian slime devil is marine fish and small aquatic and terrestrial mammals, they have been known to attack humanoids when they feel their territory has been invaded or their eggs are threatened.

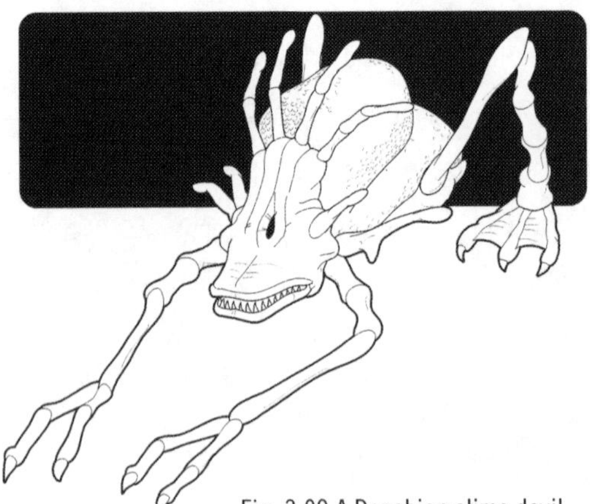

Denebian slime devils will often attack terrestrial prey as large as humanoids, but when they do so they will strike very close to shore

Fig. 3.09 A Denebian slime devil

because their physical structure is optimized for aquatic predation and can be ungainly on land. The slime devil's preferred mode of attack is to spear its prey with its foreclaws and wrestle it to the bottom of a shallow depth of water. Once its prey is pinned on the bottom, the slime devil will tear it apart with its large rows of razor-sharp teeth. Against very small prey, the slime devil will sometimes attack first with its teeth.

If you are attacked underwater by a Denebian slime devil:

- Your first, best chance for escape is to not allow yourself to be pinned. If you have a phaser or other weapon, shoot the softer tissues of the creature's abdomen and thorax. This should be enough to force the animal to retreat.

- DO NOT aim for the creature's head. Its head carapace contains reflective minerals that can cause an energy weapon to reflect back on the shooter, and it is dense enough to cause projectiles to ricochet unpredictably.

- If you have only a hand-to-hand weapon, stab at the slime devil's abdomen and thorax, or, if those are unreachable, try to stab into the olfactory opening in the center of the creature's head carapace. Beyond that opening is a delicate mass of tissues that the creature uses to track prey. Unless the creature is extremely hungry or is defending a nest area, this should be sufficient to convince it that you pose a serious threat, and it will retreat.

- If you do not have a weapon, use your feet to kick at the creature's soft underbelly, or, if that's not possible, attack the ventral extensions of its head carapace, which are part of the slime devil's natural radar sensory system.

- **DO NOT** let your feet get too close to its mouth when you are trying to kick free. A Denebian slime devil's jaws are powerful enough to pierce through most footware and lock its fangs into bone and muscle.

If the slime devil has part of your body locked in its jaws and you don't have a weapon, your only chance to free yourself is to strike at its two vulnerable points:

- Force your fist, foot, or—preferably—a foreign object into its olfactory opening; or

- Attempt to break the ventral appendages of its head carapace.

If a slime devil pins you, you will have only a few seconds to escape before it begins clawing you apart. The creature will likely strike for your head or throat, to deliver a single killing blow. It will lift itself off you slightly as it poises to strike. In that moment:

- Bring your knees to your chest and place your feet under the creature's midsection;

- As the slime devil lunges forward, kick upward to just behind where its head carapace meets its abdomen;

- Wrap your legs around the creature's very large neck and lock them together at the knees;

- Simultaneously, punch as hard as you can into its olfactory opening; continue punching there until the creature begins to seem disoriented;

- Break as many of its radar sensory appendages as you can reach; this will disorient the creature, increasing your chances of a successful escape after you release it;

- Release the creature and swim as quickly as possible for the surface and, if possible, for the nearest shore.

3.10   DEALING WITH CHARGING KLINGON *SARKS*

The Klingon *sark* is a beast of burden used on many worlds colonized or explored by the Klingon Empire. These powerful and extremely fleet-footed creatures are similar in size and behavior to Terran horses and Talnerian riding lizards. The *sark* is an omnivorous quadruped equine life-form that measures roughly 2.5 to 2.9 meters tall at the shoulder, and mature adults weigh in excess of 340 kilograms. A *sark*'s two sharp, straight horns can extend more than a meter in front of its head. *Sarks* have coarse, shaggy coats of fur that can be various colors. Their tails are spiked, like a flail, and can strike with lethal force while the creature is charging. *Sarks* are capable of accelerating from a standstill to speeds greater than 80 kph in less than twelve seconds.

If you encounter one or more *sarks* in the wild:

- Slowly and quietly move away. Be careful not to alarm the creatures.

- Do not antagonize the creature(s). *Sarks* normally will not attack humanoids unless they are very hungry or unduly provoked.

- Avoid contact with *sark* calves or females. Approaching them will provoke males to charge.

If you find yourself in the path of a large *sark* stampede:

- Try to reach a high, concealed position and avoid drawing the herd's attention.

- If cover is not available, do not attempt to flee by anticipating the herd's direction. Your motion will draw the herd toward you. Instead, run in the same direction as the herd as fast as you are able, and do your best to run with the herd. In most cases, the herd will simply navigate around you and will quickly outpace you, leaving you free to seek cover.

If you are attacked by a single s*ark:*

- Do not attempt to face down a *sark*'s charge, not even if you have weapons. *Sarks* are very fast and powerful, and their body mass makes a spearing attack by their horns more than capable of disemboweling a humanoid in a single pass.

- Seek cover, preferably in tall trees or on high ground in rough terrain. Remain concealed or out of reach for as long as possible. *Sarks* have relatively short attention spans, and in most scenarios they will quickly become bored and walk away.

- If cover is unavailable, attempt to divert the *sark*'s attention. If nothing appropriate is at hand, run toward another possible target for the *sark,* a prey animal or even—only when no other alternative is possible—another male *sark*. When the *sark* has been diverted, move as far away as possible.

3.11 EVADING WANONI TRACEHOUNDS

Wanoni tracehounds are predatory creatures indigenous to planet Arak III. The species is now found on a variety of worlds throughout the Alpha Quadrant because it is highly prized by hunters and law-enforcement agencies, who use tracehounds to track down prey and fugitives, respectively. Wild and trained tracehounds are equally dangerous; the primary difference is that in the wild they tend to be solitary. Trained tracehounds often hunt in packs.

The Wanoni tracehound is a large canine animal, similar in general build and coloring to a Terran mastiff, with exoskeletal armor plates and venomous, spined neck frills. Although tracehounds are by no means sentient, they are extremely cunning animals and have demonstrated an ability to learn and adapt to the behavior patterns of newly encountered prey.

Fully grown adult tracehounds can measure more than two meters in length and can weigh in excess of 150 kilograms. They can run for extended periods of time at speeds of up to 70 kph. They have keen senses of smell, and their hearing extends from subaural to ultrasonic frequencies. Their vision, however, is heat-based and they are poor at tracking motion at distances of more than 100 meters.

If you are being hunted by one or more Wanoni tracehounds:

- Mask your scent immediately. Use a breathing mask or a cloth to contain your exhaled breath. Use extremely strong odors to mask your natural scent; ammonia, chlorine, and camphor work best, as they have been proved to repel tracehounds, who instinctively associate them with the poisonous plants that dominate the ecosystem on Arak III.

- If you are injured, stanch all bleeding immediately and bandage the wounds thoroughly. The scent of blood draws the tracehounds more quickly than any other.

- Mask your heat signature. Insulated garments, particularly EVA suits or cold-weather gear, are very effective at concealing heat signatures in cold environments. In warmer climes, try coating yourself in a thick layer of mud.

  Be mindful that if you are traveling barefoot over soil or pavement, you will leave noticeable heat footprints that will persist for several minutes after your passage, depending on local weather conditions and your species' ambient body temperature.

  If you are unable to mask your scent, try to limit your movements to underwater. This will help mask your heat signature and will disperse your scent over a wider area, making it more difficult for the tracehounds to zero-in on your position.

- Move slowly, and place great emphasis on moving as quietly as possible. When possible, set loud decoys that you can trigger remotely from the greatest possible distance. (For instance, a tricorder set to emit a full-fidelity recording of your voice could be set to play back when you triple-tap your combadge. Coupled with a scrap of your scent-infused clothing, such a decoy could be very effective, and could be activated at ranges of up to 100 kilometers, depending on local terrain and atmospheric conditions.)

If your attempts at escape fail and you are forced to defend yourself from a Wanoni tracehound:

- Defend your throat and abdomen; they are the

Wanoni tracehound's preferred points of attack.

- Do not try to attack the creature's throat or neck; its neck frill is very sharp and highly venomous.

- Aim for the creature's nose, eyes, and ears. Jam sharp objects into them; do whatever you must to impair the animal's senses. If you disable all its primary hunting senses and the creature persists in its attack,

- Deliver a killing blow by piercing under the scales of the lower left quadrant of its torso, where its heart is located.

If you are facing a pack of Wanoni tracehounds, seek out the one that begins circling you first; this will be the alpha male of the pack. Attack it as instructed above, but do not kill it; leave it critically wounded. The rest of the pack will then instinctively turn against it and begin an internecine battle for dominance. During this period of infighting, flee as quickly as possible, and resume the evasion tactics detailed above.

3.12   ESCAPING FROM A VULCAN *LE-MATYA*

The Vulcan *Le-Matya* is a lithe, green feline quadraped with an orange or yellow diamond pattern along its back and rings of the same color on its tail. It has three-toed paws, large fangs, pointed ears, and long black claws. Its fangs and claws are poisonous; the poison sacs containing a *Le-Matya*'s nerve toxin are located inside the central pads of its paws and at the base of its jaw.

The *Le-Matya* is one of the most fearsome feline predators in the Alpha Quadrant. *Le-Matya* frequently attack multiple targets and prey larger than themselves, and they will aggressively hunt down other predators that encroach on their hunting grounds.

Indigenous to the Vulcan homeworld, *Le-Matya* now are found on several hot, desolate worlds. Despite attempts to prevent the creatures from hiding aboard starships, their stealth and cunning—and their ability to hide and survive long periods without feeding—make it difficult to contain this species.

The presence of a *Le-Matya* is often presaged by its shrill screech, which can be heard from up to 12 kilometers away in a normal, M-Class desert environment.

Le-Matya prefer to inhabit hot, rocky desert regions, and are often found near volcanic formations and in chaotic mountain terrain. They make their nests on high, rocky ledges and overhangs. If you encounter a *Le-Matya* nest that contains young cubs, do not touch them or any food nearby. Retreat from the area immediately. An adult *Le-Matya* will attack any creature it sees near its cubs.

Le-Matya tend to hunt near bodies of water, which act as a magnet for prey in a hot desert climate.

If you approach a body of water in a desert region and see no other creatures nearby, be especially attentive for clues of a *Le-Matya*'s presence, such as green and orange or yellow fur left on rock ledges or on sharp plant growths.

Fig. 3.12 A *Le-Matya*

Be particularly wary if the body of water is flanked by tall, rocky ledges or cave walls. *Le-*

Matya prefer to attack from above, leaping down on their prey.

If you are in a group of people attacked by a *Le-Matya*:

- Note that a *Le-Matya* is easily distracted. It will shift its attention from one target to another based on motion and the direction from which it was last attacked.

- Keep the *Le-Matya* off-balance by taking turns attacking it from a distance with thrown objects such as spears, knives, or rocks. Circle the creature constantly, and continue widening your circle until you have moved out of its territory.

If you are fleeing a *Le-Matya*, endurance is your best defense. *Le-Matya* are highly territorial and will not venture far past their marked hunting grounds.

If you are alone when attacked by a *Le-Matya*:
Inevitably, you will have to kill the creature in order to survive. *Le-Matya* kill even when not hungry, and if you are alone it will not permit you to retreat.

- Arm yourself with a heavy, bludgeoning weapon, such as an ax or a rough-edged stone. A sharp edge is helpful, but the weapon's weight and mass are more important.

- As soon as the *Le-Matya* is within striking range, strike at its head, at a point just behind its brow ridge. Your goal is to crush its skull as quickly as possible.

- Do not try to wrestle the creature or fight it unarmed. It is very fast, its fangs and claws are exceptionally sharp, and its poison is fast-acting and powerful.

If you are poisoned by a *Le-Matya*, there unfortunately is very little you can do; there currently are no known antidotes for *Le-Matya* poison.

3.13 DEFENDING YOURSELF AGAINST A KRYONIAN TIGER

The Kryonian tiger is a large and powerful feline predator found in arctic and subarctic environments. A fully grown adult male can measure up to 1.75 meters tall at the shoulder, be nearly 3.5 meters long, and weigh more than 370 kilograms. The style, length, and color of a Kryonian tiger's fur all change with the seasons, but the species tends to be bluish-white with steel-gray eyes. Their large and powerful paws are heavily tufted with fur, which conceals retractable claws of great size and hardness.

Kryonian tigers see in the ultraviolet spectrum, possess ultrasonic hearing, and are able to withstand temperatures of up to –30 degrees Celsius with no ill effects. They hunt in groups, which usually number between five and ten individuals. Both male and female Kryonian tigers hunt, and they often cooperate to flush out prey for the kill.

Because Kryonian tiger prides prowl and hunt openly on the icy plains and frozen tundra, it should often be possible to detect them from ranges of up to a hundred yards. If you see a group of hunting Kryonian tigers, take cover. Conceal your heat signature and remain hidden until the group either moves away or focuses on other prey.

If you happen upon a Kryonian tiger lair, or encounter cubs without an adult of the species present, withdraw immediately. If you encounter carrion or fresh kills near the lair, leave them untouched. As with most predator species, touching a Kryonian tiger's food and being in proximity to its young are both extremely likely to provoke an attack.

Kryonian tigers often seek out natural hot springs as lairs and places to birth cubs, and they have been known to mistake heated vessels and installations for caves containing hot springs. To avoid drawing Kryonian tigers into your vessel or encampment, keep all heated areas well insulated and sealed.

If you draw the attention of one or more Kryonian tigers:

- Back away carefully. Do not run—to a Kryonian tiger, that is an invitation for attack.

- Seek high ground or another defensible position. Do not let the pride surround you.

- If you have the time and the means to prepare defenses, do so immediately. An effective repellent is to use a communicator or tricorder to generate a series of powerful, ultrasonic pulses at frequencies between 480 kHz and 518 kHz. Pulses in this frequency range trigger a fear response in Kryonian tigers without causing any physical harm.

- Remain close to a large fire. Kryonian tigers can be kept at bay with lit torches or chemical flares, and they will hesitate to approach a large, hot bonfire.

- If you are unable to prepare defenses, or if you are surprised by a pride while asleep, play dead. Hold your breath and remain calm. Kryonian tigers do not scavenge; if it believes you are dead, it will move on.

If you are attacked by a Kryonian tiger:

- Lie flat on your back and draw your knees up to your chest to protect your abdomen; use your arms to protect your head and throat. Kryonian tigers prefer to use their powerful jaws to break the neck of their prey. Do not expose the back of your neck to an attacking Kryonian tiger.

- If you have access to a chemical flare (or another source of fire or extreme heat), use it at point-blank range to burn the creature anywhere on its body or head. Except in the most extreme cases (starvation or defending its young), this should be sufficient to convince the creature to retreat.

- If you have no fire or heat-based attacks at your disposal, use tools or other handheld weapons to strike at the Kryonian tiger's snout or eyes.

- As a last resort, try to reach water. Kryonian tigers have limited swimming ability, but they cannot hunt effectively in water. Although immersion in arctic waters poses a serious risk of hypothermia, it may present your best chance for escaping an otherwise fatal attack by this enormously strong predator.

3.14 PROTECTING A STARSHIP FROM AN ALPHA OMICRON CREATURE

An unusual and possibly unique spaceborne species, presently designated only as Alpha Omicron creatures, currently make their home in the asteroid belt of the Alpha Omicron system.

An Alpha Omicron creature is a being composed of an asymmetrical plasma energy field surrounded by an outer skin of silicates, actinides, and carbonacaeous chondrates.

Fig. 3.14 Example pf an Alpha Omicron creature

The species is believed to be moderately intelligent, and its members are thought to be capable of communicating with one another by means of naturally modulated, high-frequency RF signals. The species feeds on asteroids rich in kefnium, which is a compound abundant in the creatures' outer skins.

Adults of the species are quite large; they can measure more than 600 meters in length and have a mass of more than 3,500,000 metric tonnes. They also can pose a serious hazard to spacecraft. An adult can generate an energy damping field strong enough to disable a large starship, and it can emit massive doses of lethal gamma radiation.

Immature members of the species, particularly new-borns, pose a different hazard. If one becomes separated from its parent and is outside its asteroid field habitat, it might "imprint" on a passing starship, and begin to treat the vessel as its nurturing parent. The infant Alpha Omicron creature will attach itself to a starship's hull at a point close to the power transfer nodes that link the matter/antimatter reactor assembly to the primary fusion reactors. It will then proceed to drain massive amounts of power from the vessel, threatening life-support and other critical systems.

As the newborn creature becomes stronger, it will attempt to drain ever-increasing amounts of power from the starship. If it is not "weaned" from the vessel within a matter of hours, the ship will be completely drained of power reserves and might subsequently be devoured by the still ravenously hungry newborn Alpha Omicron creature.

If an Alpha Omicron creature is encountered, and the creature exhibits aggressive behavior, the standing directive for all Federation vessels is to retreat at the best possible speed. If the creature attacks and it becomes necessary to take defensive measures, the use of weapons is strongly discouraged. Even on a minimum setting, a single phaser discharge can be lethal to an adult of the species. Because this species might be sentient, nonviolent tactics are the preferred defensive response.

Fortunately, a proven method has been established. To repel an adult Alpha Omicron creature without inflicting any harm on it:

- Initiate a minimum-level power transfer beam on a wide dispersal setting. The creature should willingly lock on to the power transfer beam as a means of draining energy from the vessel.

- Normal matter and energy in our universe vibrates on a radiation bandwidth of 21 centimeters. Adjust the radiation band vibration of the power transfer beam gradually downward to "sour the milk."

- Do not lower the radiation band wavelength too

quickly. If it changes too rapidly, the creature will launch a potentially lethal radiation attack.

- Continue to reduce the radiation band vibration until it reaches a wavelength of 0.02 centimeters. This setting has been documented to be the threshhold at which the creature will retreat from further contact.

Once the creature retreats from contract, withdraw at the best possible speed.

Because current evidence suggests that Alpha Omicron creatures might be intelligent—and therefore sentient—any encounter with the species is subject to the restrictions of the Prime Directive. The Alpha Omicron system, currently under Federation jurisdiction, is currently interdicted to all traffic, and the asteroid belt in particular has been designated a restricted zone.

Although the species has not yet been encountered outside the Alpha Omicron system, it is believed there might be other groups, or "pods," of the creatures in other kefnium-rich locations throughout the Galaxy. Consequently, unexpected future encounters with the species are still a possibility.

A team of top xenobiologists and exozoologists from the Daystrom Institute and the Vulcan Science Academy are currently working in the Alpha Omicron system, seeking to decipher the bizarre high-frequency RF signals the Alpha Omicron creatures use to communicate. Although attempts at interpreting their language—or even verifying that it *is* an actual language—have so far been inconclusive, efforts to make peaceful contact with this intriguing species are continuing.

4.0

EXTREME SCENARIOS

4.00   INTRODUCTION

Most Starfleet standard protocols for crisis situations are predicated on the assumption that you are in Federation territory, or otherwise close to assistance; and that some or all of your standard systems and equipment are functioning within normal parameters. The following section has been written to address the kinds of scenarios in which you will likely be isolated with damaged equipment or no equipment, located in a hostile or unfamiliar region of space, or otherwise cut off from outside assistance.

Some of the protocols detailed in this section have proved useful to Starfleet personnel several times (chapters 4.01–4.05, 4.12), while others deal with scenarios that have been documented only a handful of times—or sometimes only once—in the history of Starfleet.

While many of the threats detailed in section 4.0 appear to be unusually specific in origin, and their solutions highly technical in nature, it should be possible to use them as a point of reference to address situations and crises not yet anticipated or documented. Applying these protocols effectively will often require innovative approaches to the configuration and application of standard-issue equipment and systems, and an ability and willingness to comprehend concepts that are often nonlinear, nonintuitive, or both.

4.01   LANDING AND EVACUATING CRIPPLED SMALL SPACECRAFT

Because of redundant safety features built into most modern spacecraft, it is possible even for nonpilots to safely land damaged vessels, provided they follow a few simple guide-

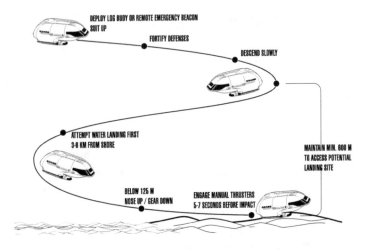

DEPLOY LOG BUOY OR REMOTE EMERGENCY BEACON
SUIT UP

FORTIFY DEFENSES

DESCEND SLOWLY

ATTEMPT WATER LANDING FIRST
3-8 KM FROM SHORE

MAINTAIN MIN. 800 M
TO ACCESS POTENTIAL
LANDING SITE

BELOW 125 M
NOSE UP / GEAR DOWN

ENGAGE MANUAL THRUSTERS
5-7 SECONDS BEFORE IMPACT

Fig. 4.01 Flight schematic for a forced shuttle landing

lines. These instructions presume that the reader is not a trained pilot, the vessel is damaged or otherwise malfunctioning, and that its autopilot system is offline.

First, remain calm. Enter the cockpit and assess the situation. The pilot's station will be on your left, the copilot's position on the right. There may be other positions in the cockpit for a navigator and an engineer, depending on the type of craft and its configuration.

If the pilot—and other members of the flight crew, if applicable—are incapacitated, remove the pilot from the left seat and take your place at the controls. Take a moment to familiarize yourself with the primary flight controls:

Navigational Reference Display: Shows your position and heading relative to nearby planetary and celestial bodies. Adjust its field of magnification as necessary. When you enter a planet's atmosphere or begin an approach for landing, this display will provide such information as your airspeed, altitude, and angle of descent relative to the surface.

Manual Sequence Controls: These will allow you to manually control such flight operations as landing strut deployment, fuel jettisons, warp core ejection, etc., if the ship's built-in fail-safes are damaged or otherwise offline. This display contains readouts of your auxiliary power reserves.

X-Y Translation Pad Control: Use this to adjust the craft's heading, or direction of travel. Use the top pad to angle the nose of the craft downward; use the bottom pad to angle the nose of the craft upward. Use the left or right pads to guide the craft in those directions, respectively.

Autopilot System: Located directly above the X-Y Translation Pad and to the left of the Warp Drive Systems Control is the Autopilot System. It is activated and deactivated by double-tapping the large, square-within-a-square pad.

Warp Drive Systems Control: Use this to control the ship's matter/antimatter-powered warp drive and its subsystems. This system is used primarily for interstellar travel. This display will indicate your craft's antideuterium fuel supply.

Impulse Systems Control: Use this to adjust the power output of the craft's fusion-powered impulse drive system. This system is used for interplanetary travel within star systems, standard orbit procedures, and atmospheric flight operations. This display will show your craft's deuterium fuel supply. Note that the craft's deuterium supply is shared by the impulse and warp propulsion systems.

Emergency Override Select: Use this to bypass damaged or malfunctioning computer systems and safety interlocks to take direct control of all onboard systems.

Manual Thruster Control: Located at the upper left corner of most standard helm interfaces, the thruster control resembles the X-Y Translation Pad. It is distinguished by being set apart from other flight controls, and typically is a different color as well. It is used primarily to make minor attitude adjustments during slow docking procedures, landings, and other low-velocity operations where it is essential to maintain close proximity to other craft or objects.

Once you have assumed control of the craft:

Attempt to engage the autopilot. If it engages, signal for help and wait for rescue; if help is unavailable, administer first aid to injured crew members, then begin repairs. If the autopilot fails to engage, assume manual control of the craft.

Signal for help. If you are in friendly space and have the ability to communicate with nearby vessels or facilities, set your subspace frequency to the Federation Emergency Channel and issue a general distress call.

Reduce speed. In most cases, slowing your craft's velocity will give you more time to react to changing situations. If the shuttle is clearly damaged or suffering from malfunctions, do not attempt to engage warp engines unless it absolutely necessary.

Don't land if you don't have to. If your vessel is severely damaged, the safest course of action is to let a starship or a starbase transport you and other crew members out of the craft and tow it to safety. Do not attempt to land a damaged craft aboard a starship or starbase if they are able to assist you.

In addition, most small spacecraft are equipped with emergency transporters that can bring you safely aboard. In cases of dire emergency where molecular transport is impossible or unsafe, you can don a SEWG (standard extravehicular work garment) and spacewalk to another craft.

If signals for help go unanswered, determine whether it is safe for you to remain in space, or if you must land or evacuate the craft.

If your craft can remain safely in space and the computer's online engineering tutorials are functioning, use the warp systems control and impulse controls to bring the vessel to a stop. Follow the tutorial's repair instructions. Prioritize your repairs based on the risks they pose to the craft and crew. Stabilize critical systems, ensure life support, restore navigation, then repair other systems as necessary. Once the craft is stabilized and safe for travel, set course for the nearest vessel, starbase, or safe landing point.

If the craft is not safe to remain in space, use the helm's Navigational Reference to assess the craft's current position and heading. Headings are expressed as mathematical coordinates that represent an X-axis azimuth value (the bearing) and a Y-axis elevation value (the mark), given in degrees of a circle. The bearing is always given first. (Note: The word "bearing" is sometimes omitted in flight instructions, but the two components of a heading are always separated by the word "mark.")

Most of your navigation in a crisis scenario will be based on relative bearing, which indicates all course changes relative to the vessel's current attitude. For instance, a heading of 000-mark-0 indicates you should continue straight ahead; a heading of 090-mark-15 indicates a turn of 90 degrees to starboard, coupled with a 15-degree upward adjustment of elevation.

If the Navigational Reference indicates there are no suitable planets on which to attempt an emergency landing, and the craft is in danger of imminent destruction, you will need to abandon ship in space. This should be done only as a last resort, as the odds of prolonged survival in space are minimal.

- If the craft has a log buoy or remote emergency beacon, set it to transmit a repeating S.O.S., then release it.

- If possible, jettison the craft's munitions and fuel to

minimize the potential collateral damage of its destruction.

- Suit up with any available pressure garment, from a SEWG to an LPEG (low-pressure environmental garment) or EPG (emergency pressure garment).

- Use the craft's emergency transporter to beam out to a minimum safe distance of six kilometers.

- If the craft has no transporter, or if the transporter is offline, use a force field to prevent depressurization as you open the craft's largest outer hatch. Open only one hatch; this will allow you to control the direction of the escaping air, and prevent the evacuees from being pulled in more than one direction. If it is not possible to generate a force field, first depressurize the cabin, then open the outer hatch.

If the force field is functioning:

- If the hatch opening is large enough for all evacuees to fit through, stand side by side in front of the hatch, but do not touch the force field. Tether all evacuees together using cables on the pressure suits. If the opening is narrow, or there are multiple evacuees, stand single-file, with each person wrapping their arms around the waist of the person in front of them. Deactivate the force field and let the explosive decompression eject you to a safe distance from the craft.

If no force field is available:

- Tether all evacuees together using the standard cables on the pressure garments, and exit the craft one person at a time. Gather on the outer hull of the craft. Using standard spacewalk techniques, propel yourself as a group, in unison, in the same direction away from the craft.

If you choose to attempt an emergency landing on a planet:

- Suit up. Don any available pressure garment—a SEWG, LPEG, or EPG.

- Fortify your defenses. Use the Emergency Override to transfer all power from weapons and nonessential systems to the craft's shields and structural integrity field (SIF). If shields are offline, divert all available power to the SIF. It will be crucial to holding your vessel together during impact.

- Evaluate your landing choices. As you near the surface, use the impulse control to reduce your forward airspeed while you survey the area. Descend slowly, at a shallow angle. You will need to be at an altitude of approximately 600 meters to accurately see and assess the terrain or water below.

- Your safest choice is a water landing. Try to find moderately deep water within three to six kilometers of shore. If a water landing is not possible, aim for empty, level surfaces, and try to find any terrain that might offer a cushion to soften impact, such as swampland, deep snow, or sand dunes.

- Pilot into the wind. Landing into a headwind will offer you better control of your descent, and it will act as a built-in braking mechanism as you seek to reduce airspeed. If you are landing on water, descending into the wind will help you touch down on the backside of the waves, making it less likely you will land into a swell that can swamp your craft.

- Keep your nose up. Once you have selected a landing target, begin a slow descent. Once you drop below an altitude of 125 meters, angle the nose of your craft slightly upward, approximately 5 to 10 degrees, and reduce airspeed to less than 200 kph. As you look out your cockpit window, the upward angle of the nose of the craft should obscure the horizon. If your craft employs landing gear, lower it now.

- Reduce power just before landing. Approximately five to seven seconds before your craft touches down onto either land or water, power down the impulse engine and engage the manual thrusters in half-reverse and full lift by single-tapping the down pad and maintaining pressure on the center pad.

- Bail out immediately after a water landing. Your craft will most likely begin to sink almost immediately after splashdown. Evacuate the craft as quickly as possible. Use your pressure garments to extend your survival time in the water as you head for shore.

- Use your craft as shelter if possible. In the event of a successful emergency landing on solid ground, determine whether your craft is structurally intact. If it poses no imminent danger of fire, explosion, or radiation and is relatively intact, use it as a shelter. It will offer adequate protection from most natural environments, and it will also be the first place that rescue teams will look for you.

  However, if you are in hostile territory, it will also be the first place the enemy looks for you. In that case, salvage all usable supplies, weapons, and materials from the craft and evacuate the area immediately. If the craft still has deuterium reserves available, set the self-destruct mechanism. This will prevent the craft from being captured and conceal evidence of your survival and departure.

If your craft suffers structural integrity failure during descent, you must evacuate immediately. If you are still in the upper atmosphere, use the craft as a reentry shield to protect you from thermal effects. If possible, wait until thermal effects subside before abandoning ship.

If the craft has a rear exit hatch, angle the craft into a steep descent; prepare to use the emergency release to blow the rear hatch. Deactivate onboard life-support systems. Assume a protective position, making certain to use your arms to protect your head and neck. Blow the rear hatch. Allow the explosive decompression to pull you and the other crew members out of the craft. Once clear of the craft and the hatch debris, employ standard freefall techniques.

If the craft has only a side exit hatch, level the craft's flight path once it clears the upper atmosphere. Find something to hang on to, then prepare to open the side hatch. When the hatch is opened, the force of decompression may pull all occupants and unsecured items rapidly to—and even through—the door. Secure all objects, and make sure all occupants have a secure hold and that the force of decompression will not pull them into other occupants, creating the risk of severe injury. Decide on an order of exit. When all is ready, open the hatch, and in order, make a free jump out of the craft, being careful to avoid such obstructions as warp nacelles or other hull protrusions.

Once in freefall, aim for deep water within three to six kilometers of shore. See section 1.11, "Surviving Atmospheric Reentry in a Pressure Suit," for further information.

4.02 SURVIVING IN AND ESCAPING FROM DAMAGED TURBOLIFTS

There are a wide variety of situations in which a turbolift can become damaged or stuck in transit, ranging from attack on a vessel or starbase to power failure, sabotage, or simple mechanical malfunction. In all cases, there are simple, easy to remember protocols you should observe if you become trapped in a damaged turbolift.

Wait a moment, then call. If you are inside a turbolift that stops suddenly and loses main and auxiliary power, remain calm and wait a few moments to see if it resumes normal operation. If power is not restored after a few moments, use the main control panel to signal for help.

If help is coming, stay put. If your call for help is acknowledged, stay inside the turblift and do not climb outside into the turbolift shaft. If you are outside when the turbolift resumes normal activity—or when a second turbolift arrives to link with yours to effect a rescue—you will suffer grievous injury and very likely death as you are either pulled into the turbolift shaft or crushed by the second turbolift car. Wait for the turbolift to resume normal operation, or for the arrival of qualified rescue personnel.

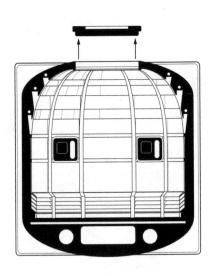

Fig. 4.02a Turbolift, with escape hatch

If no one responds, assess the risk. If the turbolift remains offline for more than a few minutes and there is no response to your requests for help, you will need to assess the safety and stability of the turbolift. If the turbolift stopped without incident, it most likely is fully secure.

However, if the turbolift's sudden stop was preceded by other signs of damage or system failure—such as a brief moment of freefall, or a fire or other hazard—there may be collateral damage that poses a continuing hazard.

Listen carefully. If you hear sounds of groaning or grinding metal from outside the turbolift car, they could be a warning that severe stress on the turbolift's emergency braking clamps is causing them to warp or slip. Other sounds to be wary of include shrieking, high-pitched whistling noises, which can indicate that a turbolift shaft has been compromised and opened to vacuum, or muffled acoustics from outside the turbolift, which can indicate the shaft is flooded with fluid or dense gas.

Check the top hatch of the turbolift. If it feels particularly hot or cold to the touch, don't open it. Extreme heat might mean there is a plasma fire in the turbolift shaft; opening the hatch will cause all the oxygen in your turbolift car to be pulled out to fuel the fire. If it's cold, the shaft might be exposed to space or flooded with dense gas or fluid.

If you can, check the turbolift's external systems. If you have

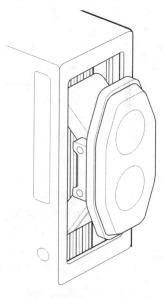

Fig. 4.02b Closeup of the turbolift's magnetic clamp

determined that it's reasonably safe to do so, open the top hatch of the turbolift. (Aboard most Federation vessels, the hatch is opened by rotating it clockwise and pushing it upward.) If there is any sign of potentially toxic fumes or gas entering the turbolift as you begin to open the top hatch, reseal it immediately.

Climb out of the turbolift car just far enough to see the two sets of emergency braking clamps, located 180 degrees apart on the sides of the turbolift car. If both are intact, your turbolift is very likely secure. If the emergency braking clamps have been compromised, and you have not been able to signal for help, you might have to evacuate the turbolift immediately.

Look up. Try to determine if there is another turbolift car trapped in the shaft above your own. If you can see one above you, determine whether its emergency braking clamps are intact. If the turbolift above you is secure, and yours is also secure, remain where you are. If the turbolift above you is in danger of freefalling, evacuate your turbolift regardless of its status. The impact of one turbolift freefalling onto another will be sufficient to destroy both.

Use ODN cable to link multiple evacuees. If more than one person needs to evacuate the turbolift and climb to an access door in the turbolift shaft, the climbers should link themselves together for mutual safety. The most readily available means of doing so in this scenario is to salvage a large quantity of ODN cable from the turbolift control panel.

To access the inner workings of the control panel, locate the override interface, tap the yellow pad once, then press the orange pad twice. This will unlock the front of the control panel. Lift it up, reach inside, and pull out as much ODN cable as possible. Loop it around each climber's waist.

Exit the turbolift in an orderly fashion. Evacuees should assist each other in climbing out of the turbolift. Once all passengers are

---

safely out of the turbolift, locate the emergency shaft ladder, and begin a careful, methodical climb to the closest turbolift door. Depending on the number of evacuees, separate your two strongest climbers; place one of them at the front of the group, the other at the rear.

Look for the nearest exit. Most turbolift systems have emergency manual releases for each set of doors. These emergency releases are sometimes hydraulically powered, and should continue to function in all but the most extreme of disaster scenarios.

Aboard starships and starbases, some emergency door releases might require a command code. If you are aboard a Starfleet vessel on which you serve, your personal code will be able to authorize any turbolift door emergency release.

Turbolift systems on many alien vessels and space stations have emergency exits at the top and bottom of each shaft that require no security code authorization. Those exits lead to isolated compartments with hard-wired communication lines to the security office.

If the turbolift car freefalls while you are inside, you will have to act quickly. Drop to the floor in the center of the turbolift and lie flat on your stomach, with your arms around your head. This will help distribute any force of impact throughout your body rather than concentrate it in any one area.

The turbolift will likely collapse if it impacts the bottom of the shaft after a long fall. Lying flat will reduce the risk of you being crushed when the turbolift's internal volume is reduced. The odds of surviving a turbolift freefall depend heavily on external factors. In a flooded shaft the risk of freefall is greatly minimized, because the drop will compress the fluid below and reduce the turbolift's downward velocity. If the shaft is exposed to vacuum, there is a risk the turbolift could widen the rupture and break free of the shaft, tumbling out into space. If a freefalling turbolift strikes other turbolifts or debris, they could serve to break its fall, but they might also result in a disastrous impact that could break the turbolift apart and kill its occupants. These risks should be taken into account when choosing a course of action.

4.03   ESCAPING FROM A MALFUNCTIONING HOLODECK

Although the holodeck has established itself as a versatile and generally reliable system for both training and recreation, a number of unfortunate incidents during its first decades of use aboard starships and space stations have made it clear that holodecks, when they malfunction, can be very dangerous.

General information about holodecks. Holodecks are equipped with numerous safety features. These range from such software-based safeties as Mortality and Injury Fail-safes—which prevent the holographic simulations from inflicting harm upon the system's living participants or allowing them, through inaction, to come to harm within the simulation—to the system's built-in limitation of molecular-level resolution, which prevents it from creating living organic matter. (Some later holodeck systems have been upgraded to include replicator emitters capable of creating actual matter that will persist even when removed from the holodeck.)

Because holodeck programs draw upon numerous information sources to create their highly realistic simulations, holodeck systems are vulnerable to damage from a variety of external sources. Some past causes for serious holodeck malfunction have included power surges; alien sensor beams that disrupted the holomatrix generators; general computer failure; and corruption of the holodeck program database.

Watch for warning signs of holodeck error. One of the most obvious signs that a holodeck program has become corrupted is a mechanical malfunction of the holodeck doors, which will open and close unpredictably. Another sign is operational failure of the control arch—for instance, if it doesn't appear when called for, or fails to accept commands. Other easily recognized clues would be inconsistencies in the program's visual matrix, which are caused by failures in the emitter system; déjà vu-style program errors, in which elements of the program seem to "hiccup," or repeat suddenly without explanation; and most seriously, "program bleed," in which elements of one holodeck program appear spontaneously in a different, wholly unrelated program. (For example, the Orient Express locomotive suddenly rumbling through a setting of Shakespeare's *The Tempest*.)

End the program immediately. Rather than risk injury by exploring a malfunctioning holdeck program, order the computer to end the program. If the program ends, report any malfunctions to the engineer in charge of holodeck systems.

If the computer does not respond or comply, call for the exit. If the exit does not appear, try calling for the arch or instructing the computer to freeze the program. If the computer remains unresponsive, you will have to determine the nature of the error, gauge the risk to yourself and other personnel inside the holodeck, and formulate a plan for terminating or exiting the program as soon as possible.

Call for help if you can. If you can let anyone outside the holodeck know of your predicament, you will greatly improve your chances of escaping safely and quickly. You will also be able to determine whether the malfunction is isolated to the holodeck or related to a more widespread external problem. The more you know about the cause of the malfunction, the better your chances of correcting it.

Don't just "pull the plug." If you are dealing with a malfunction in an early model holodeck, do not try to terminate the program by severing the holomatrix's main power coupling. Doing so will end the program, but it will also produce a surge in the holodeck emitters, causing them to release a lethal dose of anionic radiation that will kill the personnel inside. Many holodeck systems currently in use have not yet been retrofitted to correct this design flaw, so err on the side of caution.

Gauge the risk. If the program's mortality fail-safe is still functioning, you are in little danger. Proceed with caution as you seek a means of safely accessing the holodeck's controls or power grid.

If the mortality fail-safe is offline, you could be in much greater danger, depending on the nature of the program in which you are trapped. In a relatively benign program, the absence of the mortality fail-safe might not even be detected. However, a holodeck malfunction can radically transform even the most innocuous of simulations into deadly threats, so be cautious.

Diagnose the nature of the malfunction. Is it an erratic malfunction that involves program bleed, a déjà vu recursive loop, or a simple case of a program locked into operation until it reaches a predetermined end result? Is it an isolated failure or part of a larger, external matter? What is the risk, if any, of stopping the program prematurely?

Erratic and looping malfunctions, as a general rule, are not "winnable"—that is, they have no preset condition which, if met, will cause the program to terminate. Except in the rarest of scenarios, these types of program errors should be ended by force.

Programs simply locked into operation often are designed to continue until a predetermined end state is achieved.

These programs can usually be made to terminate by learning their "rules," discovering the "win condition," and playing the program to its intended conclusion.

Stop the program. Regardless of the nature of the malfunction, if there is no risk connected with ending the program prematurely, there are two methods of doing so by force, provided you have the necessary equipment.

The first method requires a tricorder. Set it to filter out the holographic matrix, then use it to locate the center of the holodeck. There you will find the floor panel that leads to the holodeck power grid relay. Reveal the access hatch by setting the tricorder to emit a low-frequency inversion field to divert the holographic projections. Realign the power relay flux capacitors to depolarize the holodeck power grid. This will shut down the holomatrix without destroying it.

The second method requires a phaser (a *real* phaser, not one generated on the holodeck). Reconfigure the emitter to generate an inverted photonic pulse and start firing in all directions, at roughly eye level. The beam will disrupt the holomatrix, causing severe damage that will be detectable by errors in the visual matrix. Continue firing until you reveal the exit. Proceed to the exit and open the emergency hatch next to the door. Pull the hydraulic emergency door release and exit.

If you can't shut it down, play it out. There might be scenarios in which it is unsafe to end a holodeck program by force. One such scenario involved the storage of crew members' transporter patterns in the holoprogram's character database; ending the program would have killed the officers. Another such crisis involved a symbiotic connection between the completion of the holodeck program and the continued survival of the starship on which it was being played out; ending the program by force would have destroyed the ship.

In some cases, such as the first scenario described above,

it might actually be desirable to keep the program running as long as possible. In those cases, the trick is to learn the program's win conditions, then postpone their achievement by any means necessary—which can be far more difficult than simply fulfilling them.

Finally, one warning applies to almost all scenarios involving interaction with holodeck programs: Do not try to tell the characters in a holodeck simulation about the holodeck itself or the nature of their existence within it. Almost all holoprograms have been written to confound such attempts at anachronistic or self-reflexive disruption. In a malfunctioning program where mortality fail-safes are offline, this tactic could backfire in a very real and lethal way.

4.04   TRANSPORTING THROUGH SHIELDS

Configuring a transporter beam to penetrate through active shields, such as those used aboard starships and starbases, is almost impossible. There are some rare exceptions to the rule, such as vessels operating ultra-high-power sensor nets (which cause minor gaps in the shield cycle), but even under optimal conditions it remains an extremely high-risk undertaking. The tactics detailed here should be employed only in cases of life and death, and only after every possible alternative has been exhausted.

First, determine if the target vessel or facility is using technology such as an ultra-high-power sensor net, that causes exploitable errors in shield nutation cycles. If the target is found to be potentially vulnerable, proceed to the next step.

Match the frequency of your transporter's annular confinement beam (ACB) to the nutation of the target's shields.

Be careful to monitor the target's shield nutation frequency; tactical protocols aboard many vessels and at several starbases mandate rotating shield nutation to random frequencies at random intervals in order to thwart attacks by technologically adaptive species such as the Borg.

Once you are certain the shield nutation frequency is stable, determine the point at which it restarts its cycle. If the shield system has a gap, it usually will be between 0.02 and 0.03 seconds in duration, and it will occur at the cycle restart point. Such gaps will occur, on average, approximately every five to six minutes. It is during this brief gap in the shield cycle that you will have to target your ACB and initiate your transport rematerialization sequence.

Continue to monitor the shield nutation. Program your transport targeting scanners to automatically target the shield gap when it occurs. Forty seconds before the gap occurs, dematerialize your transport subject. (Because of the extremely short duration of the gap and the tremendous amount of energy that will be needed to maintain the ACB once the shields resume their cycle, you will only be able to transport one subject at a time.) Hold the subject in your transporter's pattern buffer while you wait for the gap to occur.

When the gap forms in the shield, initiate the transport rematerialization sequence and boost all available power to the ACB.

Warning: At this stage of the operation, there is no way to abort transport and retrieve the subject's pattern. If the target vessel alters its shield nutation during the transport rematerialization cycle, the transport subject will be dispersed and die instantly.

It also is important to note that because it will be impossible to scan for life-forms at the beam-in point, there is a pronounced risk that the transport subject could materialize in the midst of a group of hostile personnel—or literally inside the body of one or more personnel, killing all of them.

If the transport sequence is being initiated from a vessel or facility also protected by shields, it will be necessary to match your shield nutation to match that of the target. If the shield nutations are different, it will not be possible to modify the ACB to compensate for both.

Another caveat: If during transport, any set of shields being penetrated by the ACB is struck by weapons fire or otherwise severely disrupted, the resulting flux and frequency shift as the shields dimple and recover will be sufficient to disrupt the ACB and disperse the transport subject's pattern.

In addition, if any of the above tactics are employed while moving between vessels traveling at warp velocities, refer to section 4.05, "Transporting to Ships Moving at Warp Speeds," for more information.

4.05 TRANSPORTING TO SHIPS MOVING AT WARP SPEEDS

Transporting while moving at warp velocities is an extremely hazardous activity that should be attempted only in the most dire of circumstances. The subspace distortion caused by propagating a transporter's annular confinement beam (ACB) through an active warp field can scatter a subject's pattern across several light-years if done incorrectly.

The protocols for warp-speed transport are rigid and must be followed precisely.

Move as close as possible to the target site. Because it will be necessary to form a stable bond between both vessels' warp fields, the less distance there is between the origin and destination the better.

Match the heading and velocity of the target precisely. In order to form a stable bond between the two vessels' subspace fields, their respective warp geometries must possess identical integral values. Failure to maintain warp field equivalence during the entirety of the transport cycle will result in a fatal loss of ACB signal and pattern integrity.

Form a subspace bond between both ships' warp fields. Adjust your vessel's warp field geometry and subspace field harmonics to match those of the target vessel. Use a low-power verteron pulse to bond both ships' warp fields.

Compensate for subspatial distortion. To alleviate the pattern degradation and signal disruption of transporting within a subspace field, upshift the frequency of the ACB by 57 MHz.

Warning: If there is any change in either vessel's warp velocity or subspace field geometry or harmonics during the transport cycle, the ACB will destabilize and the transport subjects' pattern integrity will be lost.

As a final note, if either or both vessels have their shields up during this procedure, the odds of success are greatly diminished, practically to the point of nonexistence. See section 4.04, "Transporting Through Shields," for more information.

4.06 CREATING METAPHASIC SHIELDING TO CONCEAL A VESSEL IN A STELLAR CORONA OR SIMILAR ENVIRONMENT

Metaphasic shielding is a modification of existing defense screen technology that uses a series of overlapping subspace fields to create a pocket of interphased energy. Objects within this interphased region exist partially in subspace, allowing them to move unharmed through such extremely hostile environments as stellar coronae, volatile nebulae, and radioactive gas giant atmospheres.

The primary drawback to metaphasic shielding is that it requires enormous amounts of energy, and if it is miscalibrated by even the smallest degree, it will collapse utterly, leaving a vessel completely defenseless.

To modify a vessel's standard defensive screens into metaphasic shields requires four basic steps.

- Synchronize shield emitter nutation to the warp field coil output frequency. This will be essential in maintaining a dynamic connection between the shield configuration and the generation of overlapping subspace fields. The warp field coils will generate the subspace fields, but it will be the shield emitters that shape and stabilize them.

- Reconfigure the vessel's warp field coil output using the shield geometry as a template. This will enable the warp field coils to emit the subspace field in a geometry close to its final form, minimizing the amount of energy required by the shield emitters to shape and stabilize the metaphasic shield.

- Initiate redundant safeguards in key systems. To maintain proper synchronization between the warp field coils and the shield emitters, any fluctuations in the electroplasma system (EPS) flow regulator or the shield emitter coil polarity must be minimized, and eliminated if possible. The shield generator's radial force compensator should be recalibrated against the structural integrity field base value every 110 microseconds to ensure shield stability.

- Calibrate the metaphasic frequency to the environment. Numerous characteristics of an environment, such as a stellar corona, will have an impact on the exact setting of the metaphasic shield. Adjust its frequency and geometry to compensate for higher temperatures, radiation levels, magnetospheric disruption, and gravimetric interference.

Once the metaphasic shield is active, be alert for signs of malfunction or improper calibration. Such signs include baryon particles inside the vessel, and rapid increases in hull temperature. Do not be alarmed by elevated neutrino levels inside the vessel, however; they are a normal and harmless product of the subspace shield.

Another phenomenon to watch out for is a phased ionic pulse, which can disrupt the metaphasic shield matrix. The presence of a phased ionic pulse will be indicated by the sudden formation of a tetryon field inside the metaphasic shield. It also should be noted that this is only a threat when the metaphasic shield is active; the shield components are not vulnerable to remote interference when the system is offline.

A final note: These modification protocols for metaphasic shields will not be effective in Starfleet vessels older than the *New Orleans*-class ships. Shield emitters in Starfleet vessels commissioned before the *U.S.S. New Orleans* lacked nanocochrane stabilizers in their frequency stabilizers, and consequently are incapable of maintaining sufficiently precise synchronization with the warp field coils to modulate a metaphasic shield.

Precise specifications on most classes of nonallied alien vessels are not currently available; consequently, efforts to configure metaphasic shields aboard non-Federation vessels will be, at best, a trial-and-error proposition.

4.07 DETECTING CLOAKED OBJECTS AND VESSELS AT CLOSE AND INTERMEDIATE RANGES

Locating a cloaked vessel or object in space is extremely difficult, and often requires an active search protocol using a widespread tachyon sensor net. Passive detection of cloaked vessels in space is almost impossible. In the mid-23rd century, many cloaking devices still suffered from imperfect visual refraction matrices that interacted with random tachyons and neutrinos from the vessel's warp core, causing a telltale distortion that a trained eye watching from a stationary vantage point could see moving against a starfield. Today, such visual artifacts have been all but eliminated from even the most simplified cloaking devices.

Locating a cloaked vessel or object on a planet surface can be less difficult, depending on the type of planet and what is being concealed. Some typical phenomena to scan for include the following:

- A ship's engines, sensor net and subspace transceiver all produce extremely powerful interference on RF bands between 119.5 MHz and 164.2 MHz, at ranges of up to 100 kilometers.

- Most cloaking devices, when active, are fountains of high-energy neutrinos that can be detected with a passive radiation scan in a bandwidth of 9.85 GeV.

Advanced technology is not always needed to locate a cloaked vessel or object on a planet. If the planet is a standard M-Class, with water and an atmosphere, there are numerous clues to a cloak's presence:

- You will often see deep impressions in soil caused by a cloaked vessel's landing gear.

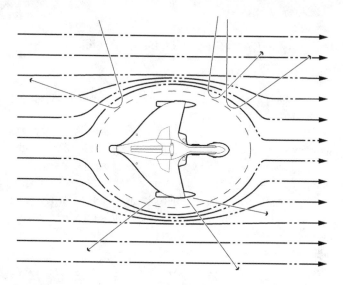

Fig. 4.07 Schematic of a cloaking field bending light around a starship, but reflecting and emitting other particles

- Older cloaks ionize atmospheric particles that contact them, producing a strong odor of ozone in proximity to the cloaked vessel or object.

- The electrostatic repulsion of a cloaking field can, and often does, permit water vapor to accrete on its surface. When the water vapor achieves sufficient volume to form droplets, it will reveal the general size and form of the cloaked object.

Detecting a vessel or object concealed by a phased cloak is essentially impossible through passive means, regardless of the environment. If the presence of such a cloaking device is suspected, the only theoretical method of detecting it is to run a high-power scan for localized subspace phase distortions that might be as discreet as 0.3 millicochranes from normal phase. However, no one has yet reported any successful detections using this method.

KNOWN TYPES OF CLOAKING DEVICE

At present, there are two known types of cloaking device. The first type works by bending visible light, masking heat, and passive radiation, and refracting most active scanning beams.

Earlier, more primitive models of this basic cloaking device had such flaws as creating electromagnetic echoes, or were undermined by ship design flaws, such as failing to suppress plasma exhaust trails. Cloaks aboard the obsolete D-12 series of Klingon birds-of-prey contained defective plasma coils that could be triggered by a low-level ionic pulse. Triggering the cloak to activate would lower the bird-of-prey's shields and power down its weapons, rendering it vulnerable to attack.

Although those early flaws have long since been corrected, many cloaking devices can still be detected even in interstellar space through the use of active tachyon sensor nets.

The second type of cloaking device, a phased cloak, is still in its early, experimental stages. A phased cloak uses subspace field manipulation to shift a vessel out of phase with normal matter, rendering it all but impossible to detect through conventional means. A vessel shifted in this manner is also capable of passing through solid matter unharmed. Despite some catastrophic early setbacks, research into this frightening new technology is still being pursued by the Romulan Empire.

Once a cloaked object or vessel is detected, collapsing its cloaking field is an even more difficult challenge. Theoretically, an inverse ionic pulse could destabilize a cloaking field matrix, but it would have to be precisely calibrated to the cloak's neutrino field frequency, and it would have to be more powerful than the cloaking field amplitude by approximately 1,000 percent.

The current theoretical model for destabilizing a phased cloak calls for a massive bombardment of anyon particles, in a localized field strength equal to nearly 10,000 times that of the cloaking field. To force a phased warbird back into normal space-time would require an anyon field with the combined maximum power output of four *Sovereign*-class starships.

4.08 REVERSING RADICAL SUBSPATIAL COMPRESSION

The first question that many explorers of deep space ask when confronted with this phenomenon is, "What is it?" Simply put, it is the effect caused by a rare, naturally occurring subspace anomaly that reduces the physical size of objects by compressing the distance between the subatomic components of its constituent atoms. The one documented subspace compression anomaly within Federation space has been shown to reduce objects to as little as 1 percent of their original size.

The causes of subspace compression anomalies are not fully understood, but some theoretical models indicate they might be the product of the fusion of a black hole and an antimatter black hole, or the intersection of a subspace fissure and a temporal distortion.

Subspace compression anomalies are easy to detect. Most subspace compression anomalies are detectable from across interstellar distances, and they should be avoided if at all possible. The one documented anomaly in Federation space has been marked by Starfleet warning buoy Delta 917-Kilo.

Do not enter the anomaly alone. If you must enter a subspace compression anomaly for whatever reason, take the precaution of having a second, larger vessel remain outside the anomaly's area of effect—known as its accretion disk—and keep a tractor beam locked on to your vessel. In the event of an accident or sudden instability in the anomaly, the second

Fig. 4.08 Effects of subspatial compression

vessel can tow you out along your original entry trajectory.

Proceed slowly. After you cross the threshhold of the accretion disk, it is important for you to maintain a precise and consistent trajectory as you move closer to the center of the anomaly. Reducing your speed to minimal levels will increase your control over minor attitude adjustments.

Watch for gamma ray flux. Gamma ray flux values will increase as your physical structure becomes compressed at the subatomic level. This is a normal side effect of the change in your physical state's inherent energy potential, and poses no serious risk to your vessel or crew. Calibrate your sensor net to use the level of gamma ray flux as a meter of the anomaly's compression effects upon your ship and crew.

Do not pass through the anomaly's center. Traveling all the way through the anomaly will cause your ship to exit the phenomenon permanently compressed. If the anomaly was particularly powerful, it is theoretically possible that you might be reduced to near microscopic size, which will make it essentially impossible for you to make a return journey through the anomaly to reverse the effects.

If you exit the anomaly in a compressed state, stay inside your vessel. Once compressed, you will not be able to breathe in uncompressed atmosphere—the molecules outside your vessel will be hundreds of times too large to be assimilated by your hemoglobin.

Monitor incoming signals and call for help. Despite your compressed state, you will be able to receive most signals normally. However, because of the reduced energy potentials of your compressed form you will be unable to transmit coherent subspace signals more complex than simple audio.

Exit the anomaly along your precise entry trajectory. To reverse the effects before passing through the anomaly, simply reverse course and follow your original trajectory out. It is important that you retrace your original flight path precisely as you exit the anomaly. Doing so will reverse the effects of subspace compression. Failure to follow a precise exit trajectory from the anomaly will cause your vessel to decompress at inconsistent rates, resulting in catastrophic subspatial shearing that will tear your vessel apart.

If you have already passed through the anomaly and exited compressed, you must re-enter the anomaly through its vertex point and retrace your original trajectory out of the anomaly. Because of your vessel's reduced thruster power, you will require the assistance of a larger vessel using a tractor beam to guide your ship out and maintain heading stability while you decompress. However, if your vessel has been reduced in size to less than 10 cubic centimeters of volume, it might not be possible for another vessel to maintain a tractor beam lock. In such an instance, your best chance is to attempt to navigate your own path through the anomaly and hope that an allied vessel can lock a tractor beam on to your ship as it begins to decompress—and before it veers off course.

4.09   PROTOCOLS FOR CONTAINING AND TRANSPORTING A PROTOUNIVERSE

A protouniverse is a newly formed universe that has formed a physical manifestation in our own cosmos. A protouniverse's presence in our universe is often microscopic; it takes the form of a subspatial interphase pocket, which bulges into our physical universe like a blister.

Interphase pockets are exceedingly rare; when they occur, they tend to be found in deep space near ultra-high-gravity phenomena. Theoretical models of naturally occuring subspace interphase pockets indicate they most likely persist in our universe for less than 100 years before being reabsorbed into subspace or collapsing in on themselves.

Because of the nature of warp field geometry, subspace interphase pockets are drawn powerfully toward active warp fields and will embed themselves in warp coil emitters. Once in contact with a warp field the interphase pocket will destabilize, causing the protouniverse contained within to expand into our universe.

If you detect a subspace interphase pocket before impact, avoid it. Drop out of warp speed and recalibrate your warp field to an inverse harmonic value to that of the interphase pocket. Doing so should negate the phenomenon's attraction to your ship's warp coils. Generate a low-level subspace field of approximately 250 millicochranes and watch for signs of movement by the interphase pocket. If it does not move toward your warp coils, leave the region at low warp. If it resumes moving toward your warp coil, continue to alter your warp field harmonics until the anomaly is no longer drawn toward you.

If it collides with your vessel, shut down warp power. The longer the anomaly remains exposed to an active warp field, the greater the risk it will destabilize and initiate an irreversible expansion of its protouniverse. After impact, the protouniverse will remain anchored to any available source of subspace distortion (such as a warp coil), but the subspace interphase pocket will remain stationary once the protouniverse has been dislodged from it.

Gather information about the anomaly. A true subspace interphase pocket will resist most normal scan protocols. To acquire accurate data, recalibrate your sensor net with a gravimetric microprobe, then run a phase variance analysis and a complete spectral profile. A protouniverse will possess some or all of the following characteristics:

- Has a high intrinsic energy potential

- Exhibits universal expansion patterns

- Appears to defy known laws of time, space, thermodynamics

Furthermore, a protouniverse that exhibits irregular, large, localized entropy decreases may very likely contain intelligent life existing on a different scale of space and time from our own. Be aware that in such cases, the Prime Directive applies to any interference in the normal development of the protouniverse or its occupants.

If you can move it safely, put it back. Returning the protouniverse to its subspace interphase pocket will contain its expansion and restore it to its natural state of development. If you are going to move the anomaly with a transporter, be certain to compensate for phase variances in the protouniverse's energy matrix. If the anomaly needs to be brought inside a

Fig. 4.09 A protouniverse

vessel or facility, Level Three containment protocols are rec-ommended.

If you can't put it back, create a new interphase pocket. If the original interphase pocket from which the protouniverse was removed is no longer extant or reachable, a theoretical alternative is to create a new interphase pocket through the controlled implosion of a pair of synchronized, high-energy subspace fields. The fields would need a strength of at least 4,900 cochranes each before the controlled implosion is triggered by the introduction of a quantum singularity at the exact moment of harmonic synchronization between the two fields.

Destroy the protouniverse only as a last resort, and only if it does not contain life. Because protouniverses can evolve in unpredictable ways and develop intelligent life on a moment's notice, benign solutions are the preferred method of dealing with this unusual and intriguing phenomenon. However, if a protouniverse is permitted to expand unchecked into our own cosmos, it will eventually supplant our universe and destroy it. Furthermore, if the expanding protouniverse is composed of antimatter, its expansion into our physical reality eventually will trigger the mutual annihilation of both.

If the entropy level in the protouniverse is found to be constant or increasing, and all attempts at benign containment have failed or proved unattainable, contain the protouniverse in a containment force field powerful enough to resist the protouniverse's next projected expansion. As the protouniverse is prevented from expanding, the feedback pressure from the force field will create an implosive wave that will collapse the protouniverse, causing it to self-destruct.

At the moment of implosion, you should expect concussive effects and severe shock waves. The magnitude of collateral damage caused in our universe by the implosion will be exponentially proportional to the size to which the protouniverse was permitted to expand before it was collapsed.

4.10   DISPERSING ROGUE SOLITON WAVES

A soliton wave is an extremely powerful, nondispersing wavefront of artificially created subspace distortion. Although there is no known natural source of soliton waves, it is theoretically possible they could be created naturally from a subspace quasar.

One of the most dangerous attributes of a soliton wave is that because it attracts soliton particles in subspace, it can actually *increase* in size, velocity, and power as it crosses interstellar distances. A soliton wave that crosses a wide

Fig. 4.10a Illustration of a soliton wave

interstellar gap, such as between the arms of a spiral galaxy, could accumulate enough power to obliterate a planet or even a star on impact.

Report all soliton waves immediately. In accordance with interstellar law, all soliton waves must be reported immediately on all emergency channels. The position, heading, and velocity of the wave should be included in the report.

Destroy it as quickly as possible. If you are in a vessel with appropriate armament and are capable of overtaking the soliton wave, you are required by interstellar law to change course to intercept the wave and attempt to disperse it. If your vessel is not armed or is incapable of intercepting the soliton wave, leave the sector immediately after filing your report of the soliton wave.

Use photon torpedoes, quantum torpedoes, or other antimatter-based munitions to disperse the wave. The soliton wave can be disrupted and dispersed by creating a "backfire" in front of its flight path.

The larger and more powerful the wave, the more powerful the explosive force required to dissipate it will be. Because most known warhead delivery systems are not structurally able to withstand unshielded passage through a soliton wave, the warheads will need to be fired from in front of the wave.

The detonation of such a large volume of antimatter munitions, coupled with the high-energy radiation released by the wave's dispersal, will create a powerful field of gamma and ionic radiation. If your ship will be in the area of effect immediately following detonation, evacuate areas of your vessel most likely to be affected by the radiation.

It is theoretically possible to disperse the soliton wave with an inverse resonance wave generated by a starship's warp nacelles. To accomplish this, the inverse resonance wave would have to be precisely calibrated to the inverse of the soliton wave's frequency and amplitude values. However,

Fig. 4.10b An antimatter detonation dispersing a soliton wave

because the frequency and amplitude of a soliton wave are both in constant states of flux, this theoretical solution is nearly impossible to execute in the field.

Furthermore, this method would require your vessel to initiate the inverse resonance wave from inside the soliton wave. Contact with a soliton wave, even one at moderate energy levels, has been shown to severely disrupt warp transfer coils, shield emitters, and transporters. Consequently, the disruption of your vessel's warp transfer coils while in contact with the soliton wave will make any attempt at precision modulation at best extremely difficult, and most likely impossible.

4.11   INDUCING SOLAR ERUPTIONS FOR TACTICAL PURPOSES

The tactical reasons for artificially generating a controlled eruption from a star's photosphere vary widely, from evading pursuit to destroying installations in close orbit to the star, but the methods for doing so are relatively straightforward—and uniquely hazardous.

Prepare an EM pulse or a charged particle beam. The key to creating a controlled eruption of superfluid gas or solar plasma is the emission from extreme close range of a high-power electromagnetic pulse or particle beam. An electromagnetic pulse will create a less powerful eruption but one that is easier to target. A charged particle beam will generate a massive solar eruption, but control of the eruption's size and direction will be negligible.

Maneuver into the star's corona. To induce the solar eruption at the moment it is desired, the EM pulse or charged particle beam must be fired from within the stellar corona.

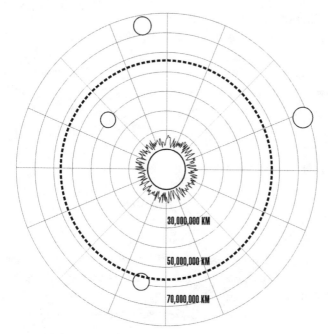

30,000,000 KM

50,000,000 KM

70,000,000 KM

Fig 4.11 The hazard zone of a created solar flare

Use an EM pulse for small, close-range targets. The best system for generating large, well-controlled EM pulses aboard most starships will be the forward sensor array.

Because an EM pulse has a lower power transfer ratio than a charged particle beam, it will be necessary to focus the pulse with great precision and fire it from a much deeper point within the corona. Consequently, the vessel firing the pulse will need to remain stationary for several seconds; normal starship defensive shields are not configured to withstand the extreme heat (in some cases, greater than 2 million kelvins) and radiation (15,000 rads per second or more) of this environment.

Even metaphasic shields (see section 4.06, "Creating Metaphasic Shielding to Conceal a Ship in a Stellar Corona or

Similar Environment," for more information) cannot withstand this level of stress for very long, but they will be your best defense while executing this tactic.

Use a charged particle beam for large or orbiting targets. Aboard most starships, the system most easily configured to emit high-energy particle beams is the tractor beam, which can be phase-shifted upward by 93 GHz to create a highly precise particle cannon.

Scan the star's photosphere to find the location of greatest magnetic instability. Be very careful when targeting the particle beam, in order to control the trajectory and volume of the superfluid gas eruption. The larger the instability you target, the larger the eruption you will generate. In order to initiate rapid subsurface fusion in the photosphere, adjust the particle beam's magnetic gradient to the inverse frequency of the instability's flux ratio.

Be aware that solar mass ejections caused by a charged particle beam can be enormous, capable of destroying ships, installations, and even small terrestrial worlds in the path of the ejection, at distances of up to 56 million kilometers.

Theoretically, a high-energy particle beam phase-shifted to match a star's gravimetric signature in subspace could induce a supernova capable of obliterating an entire star system, but the subspace distortion wave caused by such an event would prevent the ship that initiated the supernova from escaping to warp, and it would instantly collapse any metaphasic shield or phased cloaking device. The collateral effects of such an event would extend into subspace, producing a faster-than-light shockwave that would inflict damage on other star systems and vessels up to 10 light-years away.

4.12 SURVIVING WHILE ADRIFT IN DEEP SPACE

Whether you are in a starship or small spacecraft, or alone in a pressure suit, if you find yourself adrift in deep space your first priority is to transmit an S.O.S. and make every effort to continue sending it until help arrives. Your second priority is to survive until you are rescued. These guidelines will maximize your chances of doing so.

- Remain as close as possible to your last S.O.S. transmission point. This is where any eventual rescue effort will most likely begin searching for you. The closer you stay to these coordinates, the greater the likelihood that you will be found quickly.

- Conserve power and consumable supplies. Even if you are certain rescue is imminent, always anticipate the worst. Minimize power usage; maneuver spar-

Fig. 4.12 Sharing an oxygen supply

ingly, and make only those repairs essential to survival and communication. Ration and conserve all consumables—especially air, water, and food. If breathable air is limited, personnel not actively engaged in repairs or attracting rescue should sleep or otherwise minimize activity. Conversation should be limited, and hand signals or written messages should be used whenever possible.

- Consolidate your resources. Group survivors, essential equipment, and supplies together as quickly as possible. Shut down nonessential areas of the vessel, and isolate life-support functions to inhabited areas. Shut down nonessential systems and all consoles in areas of the ship that are uninhabited.

- Stay in the most secure environment available for as long as possible. If you are aboard a starship or small spacecraft, remain aboard for as long as possible before abandoning the vessel. Generally, the larger a vessel is, the longer it will provide protection from such threats as vacuum, cosmic radiation, and, in the case of a crash landing, other harsh external environments. The vessel should be abandoned only after its protective value is irreversibly compromised.

If you are adrift in a small craft, such as a shuttle, runabout, or escape pod, the following additional protocols are recommended:

- Link multiple small craft or escape pods. Joining your craft together will allow you to pool their power reserves and consumable supplies and more effectively ration all available supplies to all survivors.

- Eliminate weak links. If one or more of the linked craft or pods is too damaged to improve the survivability of the others, evacuate its personnel to the other craft. Salvage all usable parts, fuel, and supplies from the damaged craft, then set its hull adrift.

- Keep cockpit blast shields raised. In deep space, the blast shields will protect the cabin of the craft from cosmic radiation in the event of navigational deflector failure. On a planet surface, they will provide an additional layer of thermal insulation from the external environment.

- Do not make planetfall unless it is absolutely necessary. In most cases, your odds of surviving adrift in space are better than your chances of surviving planetfall in a disabled craft. You should make every effort to remain in space or in orbit until help arrives. If you are forced by circumstances to attempt a crash landing, refer to section 4.01, "Landing and Evacuating Crippled Small Spacecraft," for more information.

If you are adrift in a pressure suit, without a vessel, the following additional guidelines are recommended.

- If you are alone, send your S.O.S. and stay put. You can use your suit's built-in computer to set its emergency beacon to transmit indefinitely. Once it begins transmitting, your best chance of survival lies in minimizing your physical activity and consumables usage. Although it might seem counterintuitive, the best thing you can do is nothing. Don't talk to youself or fidget—it will only use up your oxygen more quickly.

- If you are with one or more other individuals, link yourselves together. One of the worst things that can happen to stranded spacewalkers is to drift apart in deep space. Use your suits' tether cables to chain yourselves together. This will prevent any member of your group from becoming separated by carelessness or injury.

- Share your power and supplies. By combining your suits' power and consumables supplies, you will increase the odds of all group members surviving the ordeal. The risk to individual members will be reduced by allowing everyone to benefit from the multiple redundant fail-safes of the other survivors' pressure suits. The cables and ports for joining pressure suits' O_2 and power supplies are located in the suits' chest plates. Standard-issue Starfleet SEWGs and LPEGs all have two input and two output nodes for sharing power and O_2.

- Interplex your rescue beacons to increase their range. Access the command protocols for your suits' subspace transceiver assemblies by following the prompts in your suits' forearm control interface. Interplexing the STAs for your suits' distress beacons is a standard, built-in feature of all Federation pressure suits. It will enable your distress signal to be detected at greater distances, thereby increasing your chances of prompt rescue.

- Do not make planetfall unless it is absolutely necessary. Surviving planetfall in a standard-issue LPEG or EPG is essentially impossible, and the chances of surviving planetfall in a jury-rigged SEWG are minimal, at best. This dangerous procedure should be attempted only as a last resort. For more information, refer to section 1.11, "Surviving Atmospheric Reentry in a Pressure Suit."

4.13   SURVIVING IF YOU ARE SHIFTED OUT OF PHASE

When normal matter is shifted "out of phase," it is moved out of synchronization with the rest of the space-time continuum. Depending upon how far out of phase the matter is, it might appear to unphased parties as a ghostly, apparitionlike image of itself, or it might be entirely insubstantial and completely invisible. Living beings from our space-time continuum who have been shifted out of phase have reported being able to see and hear events occurring in the regular physical universe, even though they themselves were not directly perceptible to others.

Although it is possible to temporarily shift oneself out of timephase by creating a low-power subspace force field modulated by a Type R phase discriminator set to a variance of .004 percent or greater, other phenomena have proved capable of rendering living beings out of phase permanently, and against their will. Some potentially dangerous situations of this type include:

- Activating transporter beams in, or targeting them through, chroniton fields

- Malfunctions of phased cloaking devices

- Exposure of warp phase coils to triolic waves or verteron pulses

Learn to recognize the signs of being out of phase. The farther out of normal timephase you have been shifted, the more difficult you will find it to interact with the normal physical universe. If your variance from normal timephase is less than .004 percent, you will still be able to move in a semi-normal fashion, and you will be partially visible to the normal physical universe.

If your variance is greater than .004 but less than .009, you will be invisible to those in normal timephase, and the greater your variance, the easier it will be for you to force your body to pass through objects in normal timephase. You will find it very difficult or even impossible to pick up or move objects in the normal physical universe. If you choose to pass through portals, bulkheads and other solid obstacles, be very cautious not to enter hazardous areas such as empty turbolift shafts or expose yourself to vacuum.

You will be able to interact with others who are out of phase at the same variance as yourself. You will be able to see and hear one another and interact physically.

If your timephase variance is greater than .010, you will not have to endure being out of phase for very long. Because you will be unable to interact with normal matter, you will quickly tumble through any bulkheads or planets on which you stand, and you will eventually drift into vacuum and die.

Signal for help any way you can. If your timephase variance is low and you are visible, this will be relatively easy. Indicate through sign language or communicate to someone capable of reading lips that you are out of phase and that they should collapse the timephase variance field around your body as quickly as possible.

If your timephase variance is such that you are not visible to those in normal phase, you can attract attention by going to highly trafficked areas of a ship or starbase and forcing your hands and body through solid surfaces as often as possible. When your phased body passes through normal matter, it disrupts the phase of subatomic particles in the solid surface and releases large volumes of chronitons. These collect into strong, localized chroniton fields that should draw the attention of standard internal sensors.

In most cases, anyon emitters will be deployed to negate the chroniton buildups. Exposure to anyon particles will gradually correct your timephase variance, restoring you to normal phase. To ensure that a sufficient amount of anyon particles are released to make you visible to those in normal phase, release as much phased energy as possible. Overloading a timephase-shifted phaser or disruptor to detonation will create a massive chroniton field and should draw a large response from personnel seeking to disperse it swiftly.

Concentrate your efforts on consoles where people are working, or in areas where large numbers of people gather. By staying in heavily trafficked areas, you'll improve your odds of being seen when your phase variance lowers enough to render you momentarily visible.

Be persistent. Fortunately, the effects of anyon particle exposure are cumulative, so as long as you continue to create chroniton fields and those fields are dispersed by anyon particles, you will slowly be shifted back toward normal phase.

4.14   DETECTING AND ESCAPING TEMPORAL CAUSALITY LOOPS

A temporal causality loop is a disruption of the space-time continuum in which a localized fragment of time is repeated, ad infinitum. Because the temporal causality loop is isolated from normal space-time, time continues normally for those outside the anomaly while those inside replay the same fragment of time over and over again. Consequently, a crew fortunate enough to escape such an anomaly might emerge to discover that they have been reliving the same few days—or hours—for decades or even centuries.

Although its nomenclature seems to imply that the same events are repeated identically and eternally, the fact is that not only are minor variations possible within a temporal causality loop, they are likely to multiply as the cycle repeats. Because of this potential for variation in event and outcome, it is possible to escape from a temporal causality loop once it has been detected.

Recognize the warning signs of a temporal causality loop. One frequent indicator is strong and frequent sensations of déjà vu (or, as the Klingons say, *nlb'poH*), the feeling that one is reliving events that have occurred many times before. Another common phenomenon inside temporal causality loops are audible echoes that sound like a crowd of overlapping voices. When recorded and analyzed, these chaotic sounding echoes can be identified as multiple overlapping versions of the same sounds audible throughout the ship.

Determine whether it is a short or a long loop. Longer loops are harder to detect, but once detected, they offer more time for planning and executing corrective action. It's important to react swiftly once a temporal causality loop is identified because once the loop restarts, all conscious memories of the last trip through the loop will be lost.

Shorter loops are easier to identify because they create much more powerful feelings of déjà vu—eventually, the victims adapt to a recursive temporal environment and begin to recognize their predicament much more quickly on successive repetitions. However, extremely short loops are very difficult from which to escape because they leave little time to formulate and carry out escape plans before all memory of the threat is erased.

See if you have sent yourself a clue using a dekyon field. If you have carried out the following steps during a previous iteration of the temporal causality loop, there will be a coded message from yourself in the form of a dekyon field. Locate and decipher this clue. If there is no dekyon field, then you have not yet carried out the following steps. Do so now.

Prepare a message for yourself. The only chance you will have of escaping a temporal causality loop is to learn what action causes it to repeat, and find a way to pass that knowledge to yourself during the next iteration of the loop.

Dekyons—subatomic particles with subspatial and temporal properties—are capable of crossing the event threshhold of a temporal causality loop. Use a dekyon field to transmit a clue to yourself regarding the causality trigger. Because dekyons decay quickly, the message must be very brief. It will be detectable to positronic sensors and bioneural circuit clusters.

Identify the causality trigger. The causality trigger is the event that forces the loop to restart. The causality trigger is often a highly energetic event, such as an antimatter explosion, passage through a wormhole, or contact with an anti-time disruption. The causality trigger represents the turning point at which the loop can be disrupted or restarted.

Transmit the dekyon field containing the message. This field will contain a brief clue that should register on your sensors during the next iteration of the loop.

Unfortunately, there is no known way to detect a temporal causality loop until one is already trapped inside it. The few such anomalies that have ever been documented are charted only approximately. Their precise location, size and origin are unknown. Almost all temporal causality loops ever documented have occurred in space and affected ships with faster-than-light propulsion capability.

The best-known temporal causality loop on record is located near the Typhon Expanse. It held the Starfleet vessel *U.S.S. Bozeman* in its loop for more than 90 years until the loop was disrupted by the *U.S.S. Enterprise*-D, which itself spent 17 days trapped inside the anomaly.

Keep trying. If you fail to escape from the temporal causality loop on this attempt, remember that you will get another chance . . . and another . . . and another . . .

After you escape, resynchronize your time beacon. Because you will have been isolated from normal space-time, your chronometers will be out of sync. Reset them before contacting Starfleet Command.

4.15   DETERMINING IF YOU HAVE BEEN SHIFTED INTO A PARALLEL QUANTUM UNIVERSE

There are at least 285,000 known parallel quantum universes, and current quantum theory postulates that the actual number of parallel realities might literally be infinite.

Numerous contextual clues can act as indicators that you have passed through a quantum fissure and breached the barrier between parallel quantum universes:

- Sudden, unexplained cosmetic alterations. You might notice ongoing subtle changes in your physical surroundings, wardrobe and other miscellaneous objects.

- Random shifts in context. Be alert to changes both subtle and significant in historical details of either a general or personal nature. These could include the sudden revelation that long-dead comrades are still alive—or just the opposite; political entities once well known become unknown or unfamiliar; intimate relationships seem to vanish, change, or spontaneously come into existence.

- Random translocation. Incidents of sudden, unexplained changes in position or location of yourself, other people, or random objects are a frequent side effect of slipping between quantum universes.

Confirm that you are in a parallel universe. If you observe any of the contextual clues detailed above and suspect you have been shifted out of your correct physical universe, scan the quantum spin rate and direction of matter in your cellular RNA. If you are not indigenous to that quantum reality, the quantum state of subatomic matter in your RNA will be asynchronous with that of normal matter found in that reality. This test is considered definitive because all matter resonates at the quantum level with a specific frequency. It cannot be altered or masked in any known way, and serves as the fundamental constant of reality.

For more information on how to return to your correct quantum reality and seal the quantum fissure that was breached in order to shift you into a parallel universe, refer to section 1.15, "Sealing Quantum Fissures with an Inverted Warp Field."

AUTHOR'S ACKNOWLEDGMENTS

I would first like to thank my Pocket Books editor, Jessica McGivney, for hiring me to write this book, and for not sending assassins to kill me when I started missing deadlines. This book began with her inspiration, and I am honored that she chose me to help her bring it to fruition.

I would also like to extend my heartfelt thanks to the many people whose encouragement, advice, and prodding helped me actually finish this work: my parents, David L. Mack and Yvonne Mack; my writing partner, John J. Ordover, and his wife, Carol Greenburg; Glenn Hauman and Brandy Hauman; Keith R. A. DeCandido; Bob Greenberger; all the Malibu Regulars (you know who you are); the SCI FI crew—Dan Jurow, Marlon Jackson, Michael Gerber, Michael Blancaflor, Katharine Bailey, Alissa Gordon, Ursula O'Steen, Nancy Lewis, Walter Insalata, Scott Treude, Yiram Aldouby, and Dave Lauterbach; and all my fellow *Star Trek* authors, who told me not to give up, no matter what, because I would then have to return my advance.

In addition, my thanks to John Van Citters at Paramount Licensing for his keen eye and vast knowledge of the *Star Trek* universe. His expert advice helped make this book the best it could be.

Last but not least, I offer my sincere gratitude to the many writers, artisans, and visionaries who have helped make the *Star Trek* universe so richly detailed and complex, and to Gene Roddenberry, who gave us this marvelous fictional universe to build, explore, and enjoy together.

EDITOR'S ACKNOWLEDGMENTS

I owe a massive debt to Jaime Putorti, Linda Dingler, Al Madocs, and Donna O'Neill, without whom this manuscript could never have become a book; thank you so much. Thanks also to Cynthia Mann, Lisa Litwack, and Rod Hernandez for this cover and the twenty versions the world will never see; thanks and sympathy to my author and illustrator, who worked with me as I was learning the ropes on this project; and many grateful thanks to Margaret Clark, who taught them to me (or tried her best), and without whom this project would not have been possible.